THEATRE OF WAR

First published by Charco Press 2020

Charco Press Ltd., Office 59, 44-46 Morningside Road, Edinburgh
EH10 4BF

ISBN: 9781916465657
e-book: 9781999368487

www.charcopress.com

Edited by Robin Myers
Cover design by Pablo Font
Typeset by Laura Jones
Proofread by Fiona Mackintosh

2 4 6 8 10 9 7 5 3 1

Supported using public funding by
ARTS COUNCIL ENGLAND

LOTTERY FUNDED

Andrea Jeftanovic

THEATRE OF WAR

Translated by
Frances Riddle

CHARCO PRESS

CONTENTS

ACT I

ACT II

ACT III

I do not want to be fixed, to be pinioned. I tremble, I quiver, like the leaf in the hedge, as I sit dangling my feet, on the edge of the bed, with a new day to break open. I have fifty years, I have sixty years to spend. I have not yet broken into my hoard.
This is the beginning.

VIRGINIA WOOLF

He knows why he is leery of visitors who walk his floors: thousands of unopened letters lie beneath the rugs.
ELÍAS CANETTI

ACT I

1

Private Showing

I sit in the last row. From here, the empty seats fan out like lines of tombstones. The curtain rises on the shadowy dining room of my first home. Some familiar objects: the stone statues and the flattened wolf hide. In the corner sits a table with five chairs; the one at the head wobbles. The wallpaper is stamped with faded rosettes. The spectacle of my childhood begins. Repeatedly changing houses, we are unable to anchor ourselves to any fixed point. The removal van parked along the curb, the mattresses hanging off the roof and my tricycle always at the top of the pyramid.

I sink into the plush sofa. I trace lines into the uphol-stery. I write a secret sentence on the backrest. I change my mind and rub against the grain of the fabric to erase my hieroglyphic. I hear Mum calling me from the street. My footsteps boom across the parquet; the stage trans-forms into an infinite hallway. I cross the bright threshold. Like some ritual of goodbye I take one last walk around the back garden. Wet rags are piled up on the patio tiles from the half-finished clean-up. I wipe the window of the house we're abandoning. They've left my doll Patricia at the foot of the stairs. I stand there staring at her until my mother pulls me to the car with the engine already running. I press my face against the cold back window and cry without anyone noticing.

The windows of all the houses I've lived in are super-imposed: a huge picture window looking onto a deserted street, an underground skylight, a wooden sill swollen with damp sea air, rusted iron bars framing a palm-lined avenue, a broken display window that went unrepaired for a whole year. Houses with both my parents, without my mum, with my brother and sister, with some old people I don't know. First my room on the second floor with Adela and Davor. Then a small apartment with just Dad. A narrow single bed or the wide mattress I share with Mum. Our things in bags, in cardboard boxes, in old luggage tied shut with belts. In my small suitcase I carry a photo of a neighbour who was my best friend. I keep a glass jar of dirt from all the yards I've played in.

I hate the house on the palm-lined avenue. That's where everything started... The house needs fixing up. The walls are being painted, the floors carpeted with newspaper. The doors have been stripped and everything is covered in dust. I walk through the rooms and the newspaper scrapes, crackles. I run into Lorenzo. That's the name of the workman who wanders the house dressed in overalls. He has black eyes, hairy arms, broad shoulders. As his paintbrush glides over the wall he whistles along to a tune on the radio. He says *excuse me* every time he walks into a new room. He paints the kitchen, *excuse me*, he paints the living room, *excuse me*, now my bedroom, *excuse me*. He has a sandwich in the kitchen for lunch. He takes a nap in the back yard with his shirt off. In the afternoon he puts a second coat on the walls he painted that morning. I inhale the dizzying scent of paint thinner. The workman lights a cigarette for Mum, then they lock themselves in the dining room for a long time. I picture those eyebrows framing his dark gaze. I don't have a watch, but I know it's been too long. Through the door I hear newspaper crinkling. The lock stares at me with its myopic eye. I lean against the window and count twenty-seven cars passing by on the street.

Some time later, I pick up the phone. I hear someone say to Mum *I love you* and then laugh. It's the workman. I recognise his raspy voice. Dad is brushing his teeth. I shout, I kick the walls, pull the buttons off my pyjamas. Dad rushes out of the bathroom, foaming with tooth-paste. He asks what's going on. Mum raises an eyebrow and says *just another one of her tantrums*. My heart is a drum, beating louder and louder. Bambambam. I'm possessed by a hiccup that reverberates through my chest. The rhythm accelerates. She hands me a glass of sugar water, turns off my bedroom light, closes the door. Now my sobs echo against the pillow. The ember of that shared cigarette glows inside my head. The cyclops of the dining room door stares at me, offering a one-eyed synopsis in the keyhole. The headlights of the cars passing on the street brighten one corner of my room, leaving outlines of their shapes on the wall. A truck has just imprinted its cabin opposite my bed.

Then sounds emerge from backstage. The director of the play announces that this has been a preview, a single scene. A private showing. The curtain rises and the first act begins.

2

I'm the Same Age as Dad

I'm the same age as Dad. He's stuck at age nine, which was how old he was when the war began. I don't want to get any older either. I want to stay with him in his nine-year-old sadness. Dad sleeps with the light on just like me. In the darkness, he says, the black trees might creep in. Dad is frightened by the siren at midday, when a moustached officer greets him with an outstretched arm. Dad is a six-foot-tall child, size XL, with wrinkled sleeves. I am the same age as Dad. Just that he's turned the same age several times.

Dad always has the same nightmare. He's inside an empty train station. He thinks the hand of God placed him on the wrong platform: *When I turn my head, the faces of the lost children multiply. The vacant eyes of the women. The hunched backs of the men. I clench my fists. They make the pilgrimage through this atomic landscape with their heads bowed. There are hundreds, thousands of them, shuffling between the rails. And my fists are clenched. The beings board the trains. My fists are still clenched. A shrill whistle sounds. The iron wheels begin to turn. I walk with my fists clenched. The shadows of the boxcars slither across the ground. I see them move away, their arms stretching from the narrow windows, gesturing wildly. I bound over the sleepers with my fists clenched. I watch until the darkness of a tunnel finally swallows the shapes. I run and run after the train, but it's stopped halfway, facing the wrong direction.*

Dad is absent as he reads the newspaper and thinks about the war. He does the maths, adding, subtracting, calculating the length of that period. I tell him to forget it, that there are only tin soldiers and water guns here. He says that barbed wire surrounds his dreams. Dad is stuck in time, remembering the war. A march of boots gallops in his ears. He always carries bread in his pockets. He has forbidden me to read history books; he writes a year on his leg. He doesn't know that I hide an encyclopaedia under my bed and know what that date means. He takes stock of the pantry, counts the non-perishable food items: each jar of preserves, package of rice, bag of beans lengthens his list. Every day he inventories the contents of the lockbox.

I have the urge to hug Dad and reassure him that the war is over, but we each cry alone in our own rooms. Two thousand four hundred and fifty-seven, is the number that Dad unknowingly writes on my arm the day I turn nine. This is the figure that sears my skin: the number of days that the war lasted, all the tears that Dad has cried. I commemorate my ninth birthday with four digits. I add the two, the four, the five, and the seven. I watch Dad spend the day opening and closing the newspaper. Two thousand four hundred and fifty-seven is the number of days they owe him.

From the rooftop of his childhood home, Dad watches as two soldiers knock on the door. The men speak to his mother in low voices. As he waits on the roof, he paces nervously from one side to the other. He feels the hot tar beneath his feet. From on high he watches them take his father away, arms bound. There's a gnash of fire on the horizon. He will always remember that summer afternoon when he couldn't find the voice to ask his father where he was going, what time he'd be back. He couldn't say goodbye to him either. In the following weeks he would ask every man in uniform about his dad, showing them an old photo. His boyhood muteness still drums steadily in his chest. It's the reason why he'll never again walk with a straight back. It's the reason why he moved to another country he had never even heard of.

Dad sleeps in the room next to mine, but when he closes his eyes he's lying in a cockroach-infested cellar beside his two brothers and their last fourteen cans of food. He remains perfectly still. Dad is so small that he can hide behind the wallpaper and let his eyelashes brush the wall. The three boys hold their breath because they hear strange footfalls in the hallway. The day before, they'd found the front door smashed in. The wood ripped from the hinges, a note in another language on the floor. Their mother spends hours cleaning out the closet. She shines shoes, brushes suits, folds shirts. She moves dressers and chairs. She changes the position of her bed, tidies the dining room. She wears black. At night they read the secret lists by candlelight. They do not find their father among the typed-out names. Fat drops of semen erase entire lineages.

Dad says there is a mournful rain inside him. He dreams that God kneels on his shoulder and asks him for forgiveness.

3

The Memory of the Senses

Dad as a boy, his stomach bloated with hunger. When I say *I'm starving to death*, he gets nervous and opens the cupboard. He rummages through packages, counts containers, jars and boxes. He rotates the stock. He crosses something out in his notebook of provisions. Without looking me in the eye he holds out a handful of raisins.

In Dad's city, three boxes of food could be exchanged for information. A litre of gasoline for a meeting with an officer. A family jewel for a fake passport. The streets were lit by enemy spotlights hovering over his neck on his walk home from school. The men wore tattered uniforms. They walked barefoot because they'd already sold their last pair of shoes. The dogs let out guttural growls as they rooted around in the garbage, licked the wounds of the dead. The sewers were destroyed, the toilets all leaked. Excrement on the pavements, street corners, impregnating clothes, furniture, lampposts. Intestines choked with terror. To walk on the street was to step in your own shit, the excrement of your neighbours and everyone else, all living in fear. A coagulated river of waste and faeces. The faeces flowed into the shape of an S that was intersected by Zs and Hs. A chain of excrement that snaked through the city.

I'm closing the bathroom door behind me when I hear Dad's anxious voice. I stand in the middle of the hallway, my back to him.

'Tamara, did you flush the toilet?'

'Yes,' I answer, and my legs tremble as I walk away.

'Then why does it smell like shit?'

I sniff but I don't smell anything. I know he's tormented once again by a stench that exists only in his mind. From my bedroom I hear him flush the toilet several times; the water rushes and he sprays air freshener. Dad still smells the acrid, rancid odours of his hometown. He gags from the stink lodged in his nostrils. That night I dream that I open the bathroom door and I find Dad dead, sitting on a toilet overflowing with excrement.

The kids spend their afternoons standing outside the candy shop. Dad watching at the window, as if it were a movie, caramel dripping under the heat of the lamps. The colours of the sweets form a rainbow. Through the glass, he savours a lollipop that melts in his mouth and his cracked tongue writhes. He removes the cellophane from the warm chocolates and lets them slide down his throat. But his daydreams are interrupted by the rumbling of his guts. Hunger fills his head; the cavity of his abdomen contracts. Amplifying the memory of the day's lone mouthful. A scrap of bread chewed with a few motions of his mouth in an infinite mental loop.

At the table, Dad eats quickly, not a single crumb left on the plate. He checks that all portions are of equal size. He glances sidelong at the other bowls, gathers the leftovers into his. Dad scrapes at the dish until the porcelain squeaks. Then he sops up the gravy with a piece of bread, drawing circles on the plate. He finishes before anyone else.

'Is there any more?' he asks.

'You've had enough,' Mum answers.

'Is there any more?' he asks as if he hasn't heard her.

We all sit in silence as we slowly move the forks to our mouths.

'I want more!' he insists.

Mum hands him a piece of bread, which he covers in butter and desperately devours. He hasn't even finished chewing the crust when he breaks the silence.

'Who's going to share with me?' he asks in a tone somewhere between sweet and threatening.

'But... you haven't even finished,' Mum says, nervous.

Dad carefully watches the other eaters. He rescues my leftovers, pushing them noisily onto his plate. He continues chewing after we've all finished and are slumped languidly against the table. He eats nonstop because war could break out at any minute.

When Dad looks out the window, he is hypnotised by the horizon... soldiers file by in brown uniforms that display the metal butts of their rifles. They march in double lines with their impassive faces, trailed by tanks. Dad sits on the sofa. I call out to him but he doesn't hear me. He has erected a wall of news. He reads the paper in an alphabet without history. He reads in silence as a soundtrack plays on repeat in his ears. He turns the page: he's in another time, thinking in another language. Dad is constantly invaded by the same sounds: footsteps on cobbled streets, the scrape of a shovel on pavement, the high-pitched whistle of the bombs, the death rattle of a dying man. If he keeps reading the newspaper, he hears the squeals of the train axles, the dry slam of a wooden door. Then he remembers another use for it. In his eyes, dead bodies lie on the streets, covered in sheets of newspaper.

4

Family From Another Continent

We're a captive audience. Our parents learned the art of performance on another continent. The showing begins after midnight. Dad is always delayed by his memories of the war. We all hide the same watch under our pillows, the one Mum uses to measure his tardiness. We hear his key in the door and we move to the living room. The blue plush sofa offers front-row seats. The rug is the main stage. We settle in for the show and my parents take their places. My mother wears a red robe that shows her voluptuous cleavage; her face looks gaunter without makeup. My father seems distracted, slightly more stooped, with one hand in his pocket. The wood floor creaks, the beads of the chandelier sway. Sheathed in deformed pyjamas, my siblings and I lean our heads together and our pupils dilate.

The show continues backstage. Lying in our beds, we hear Mum's shouts, Dad's hoarse exclamations. The rattle of drawers opening and closing. The floor shakes, they race around their bedroom, dented voices shuddering the walls. The foundation trembles. A movement that opens a chasm between us and within each of us. We don't want to listen to any more. We pull our wool blankets tight around our heads until we can no longer hear; our cheeks burn, our eyes fill with fluff.

We never applaud after this show. Night after night, the same scenes play out before our hollowed eyes. When everything is over, we go back to sleep. No one will speak of the performance in the morning, not that day, not ever. The only evidence is the impression left in the sofa by our bodies sunk into the cushions for so many hours. Suddenly a fleeting doubt: did we really see it or was it just a dream? We are left with phrases that float down from the upstairs bedroom like an internal echo, *leave, I don't want to see you ever again, you're a tyrant*. The words flutter, twirl, repeating over and over, threatening to drive us mad.

For a while now the refrigerator has held only a tub of margarine, half a lemon, and some empty bottles. I find three wrinkled apples in the crisper. I go into the bathroom; the flame inside the hot water heater is off, soot lining the hole like metal fangs. The pipes squeal when we turn on the hot water. Envelopes stamped with the word URGENT arrive but my parents don't open them. The school principal calls my siblings and me into her office to tell us about the unpaid fees. *My loves, tell your parents that the last chance to pay is next Friday*, she smoothly intones through painted lips. I stare at the cloth flower pinned to her dress. We leave the office, our hands scratching at pockets filled with sand and crumbs. I return home to find Dad with a pile of bills on the unmade bed, banging the keys of an old calculator.

Mum is agitated. She says *there's no money in this house, we're going to starve*. She paces back and forth as she speaks, shaking her costume jewellery. The house in complete disarray, damp towels strewn across the floor, the sink overflowing with dirty dishes, the blinds closed. Everything smells musty. Adela asks about the cleaning lady. They've fired her. The three of us look at each other and tacitly agree not to say anything about the school fees they owe. I count the money I have hidden in an empty chocolate box; it's not enough, we wouldn't even be able to survive a couple of days.

.

5

I Learn to Write by Copying
Other Kids

I learn to write by copying other kids, in a concerted effort to fill the blank page. Dad's unanswered questions guide my research into things I'll read about later. I come to answers after connecting fragments, codes, excerpts from books, old magazines, letters from family members. I lay out Dad's questions together with my findings and attempt to put the puzzle together. I look up the meaning of strange terms in the dictionary. I write down *mass grave, epidemic, deportation*. There are some words I can't find, opening a new abyss.

The things that Mum says not to say I take down in my notebook so I won't forget them. I combine words that sound good together, writing their definitions in careful handwriting. I mix long words with short ones, consonants and vowels, verbs in past and future tenses. I want to finish a sentence, but I get distracted by the latest fight. I'm still writing, I'm full of ideas. I live in a timeless space. Lost in an era that doesn't belong to me. I inhabit places I've never been. Dad, on the other hand, has never left that distant time.

Dad is still thinking about the war. He prohibits me from reading history books and scribbles a year on his legs. I record the same date like a tattoo on my brain.

One day he discovers the encyclopaedia I have hidden under my bed and says nothing. I keep searching, getting lost in other books. I run my fingertips over the drawing of that continent and I stick pins into the cities I'll visit someday. A stain on the centre of a world map. I never knew if we were from here or from there. So I founded my own country in a blue notebook where I'm not a minority. Mum and Dad want me to be ignorant. They don't want me to study, to read so much. They say that just a few words are enough; that history is for those who have no present. I copy paragraphs from books, dates, heroic figures. I witness events I wasn't present for. I come across names I've heard countless times at home. As I read, I cover my mouth to hold back my horror. I study the faces and the expressions that mask so much hate. I draw everything I think. Now I can name the places, the people, the dates that hurt me. I'm terrified to continue reading, but I need to understand my parents.

Dad and Mum come from so far away. It's visible in the distance they keep from other people. Their remote cities assert themselves through record albums in other languages, through peculiar expressions coined. At home we pray to another God, we celebrate other holidays, we speak in a language both familiar and incomprehensible to me. Our house smells different, the kitchen sweeter, the oven always warm.

In the living room there are other kinds of decorations, objects that can't be found in the neighbours' houses. There are bronze ashtrays with Turkish stones; coloured glass. A pair of candelabras on the mantle. A map with cities I don't recognise. A plaque on the left side of the door. My last name is hard to pronounce; I have to spell it out. People approach me with questions. But most of the time in the classroom or while reading

I'm not there, I choose other destinations. I want to live under a table, inside a closet, between the lines.

It's December. The neighbourhood kids are out on the streets with their new things: aluminium bikes, stylish clothes, battery-powered toys. I feel a sudden fire in the pit of my stomach. The metallic spokes rotate around the twenty-four-inch wheels. They ask about my presents; I don't know what to say. I don't have any new toys to show off. They surround me and ask why my parents talk so strangely, where their accent is from, if I've been to their country. As they interrogate me, the world spins, like when I look at the bike tyres whirling around the axle spun by the gear. I hear laughter and more laughter. Their bodies rise over their bicycle seats; they pedal fast but don't move away. They ring their bells. *Ring ring.* Their laughing floats on the air as they turn the corner. I'm standing in the middle of the street, my shadow thrown over the pavement and part of the wall. I watch myself moving endlessly over a conveyor belt. My feet tire from this lonely treadmill race.

6

Switching Roles

My sister Adela walks around the house, pale and svelte. She's thin like our mother. We're relieved when we wake up to the sound of our mother's heels leaving the house. We don't know where she's going, but her steps hammer intermittently on the asphalt. I peer through the blinds and make out spike heels, the stockings shimmering on the bridge of her foot, her ankle half covered by her trench coat. She walks decidedly towards a car. The engine starts. Adela covers our ears with the blanket so that we won't hear the night-time fights and doles out the scarce food in the refrigerator: three wrinkled apples, one egg, a half-litre of milk.

My siblings and I pretend to be each other. A game of imitation, impersonation, serving a sentence. It's the thrill of a mirror broken into cruel shards. Davor begins. He pulls a blonde wig from the trunk of old clothes and weaves it into two uneven plaits. I touch my tangled hair. He puts on a checked dress and a backwards vest. He laughs with his front teeth sticking out. I immediately close my mouth, which had been hanging open, ready to smile. He imitates my clumsy gait, my constant pout. He pulls on his eyes to make them look slanted. He puts his finger in his nose and then makes curls in his hair. He recreates one of my sobbing tantrums. I suck on my hair until the strands are stiff. Adela breaks into hysterics every time she identifies a new trait. I can't laugh, I'm too busy fighting back tears.

As if I weren't bothered, I get up on the table and improvise a scene with Davor. Adela yawns a few times and leaves. I tell him we should play *mum and dad*. I put on an apron and transform the living room décor into my kitchen utensils. *I'm your wife, the mum, and I'm going to make you some yummy food.* He utters a few words and then goes off script. His throat trembles with sobs, he bangs his head against the wall. He wants his dad, his daddy. The curtain falls, the spotlight fades. That was the day I finally realised that my dad wasn't my brother and sister's dad. Theirs had died many years before, when Davor was just beginning to walk and Adela was learning to read. I suddenly understood the different surname on Adela and Davor's school supplies, their clothing tags. I'd noticed the darker tone of their skin, their different facial features, their softer expressions. But I'd also noticed their almond-shaped eyes, their large hands, their smooth foreheads. I comprehend the silence that falls when my dad is around, why he doesn't take them to school like he takes me. I stop mentioning Dad around Adela and Davor. I feel guilty.

At night I escape to Adela's bed and we watch horror movies from our hiding place under the sheets. Psychopaths run with axes, leap out of the television screen and chase us.

'Close your eyes, don't squeeze me so tight!' she says to me.

'Ahhh, the nanny's head got cut off. Look at it dangling!' I cover my eyes.

'The nanny is the killer. She abused the baby when she took it to the park in the pram. Cover your eyes.'

'Can I open them now?' I ask.

'No, not yet. Wait... You can look now, it's over.'

Adela's horsehair brush whispers gently over my hair, as it does every night. She patiently unknots my tangles. Sometimes she makes me scream, but she manages to lull me to sleep with the purring sound of the brush that calms my anxiety, my agitated emotions. Her caress follows the curve of my neck. A shiver runs from the roots of my hair to the tips. Swirling spirals on the back of my head. While she brushes my hair, she tells me she wants to live far away, to have three kids, to study languages.

Davor, inspired by the horror movies, scares us with monstrous masks, chases us with knives. He makes terrifying sounds, he howls like a madman behind the doors. The house seems possessed by ghosts sharpening their silhouettes on the thresholds. The nightmares step into the bedroom, climb up the nightstand and over the sheets, cast themselves onto the walls. I see an enormous animal, the shadow of a deformed man in the doorway. I scream without making a sound; I sit up quickly, gasping.

'Adela, I can't sleep. I had a nightmare, move over.'

She pulls back the sheets and slides deeper into the bed.

7

Dad and My Blood

I bleed when I shouldn't. Every other day. Every Monday. I fill my drawers with cotton pads and gauze that I press between my thighs. Dad acts strange when I bleed. On those days he won't say a word to me. Our eyes meet at the table. They're so similar, our eyes. I think, when I bleed, that Dad thinks I've wounded someone. I don't remember having hurt anyone. Maybe I did, but I can't remember.

Dad says *I don't want any blood in this house*. It's the only time he pounds the table. I hide in my bedroom and hang my stained underwear on the bare bulb suspended from the ceiling. I study the world through this lens. The curtains look splattered, the window is a haematoma, the door is marbled with red. The room is lit by a scarlet light. If I close one eye, the tone ranges from maroon to crimson; if I open the other, the intense red goes pink. If I turn quickly, the lava engulfs the rug, the bedspread, the curtains. But suddenly someone knocks on the door and the fire dies out.

I'm terrified of this lava flow that threatens to destroy me. I lie in wait for any sign. I verify with my index finger that the tepid lava runs between my thighs. In the shower I use the liquid to write my name on the tiles. When I'm older, I draw a heart with Dad's name and mine. Then I cross it with an arrow. Dad sobs five days a month. My knees are numb: two blocks of ice. Dad cries nine months of the year. Something stabs at my gut. He reads the newspaper while I try to be his daughter. I'm so pale, and I have dark circles around my eyes; I don't know the name of the illness that afflicts me. Dad is nauseous, dizzy. My body feels heavy, my bones ache. Dad's abdomen inflates, grows outward. I don't know why I feel so sad. The soft mounds of his breasts swell. I try to remember the crime: the murderer, the victim, the scene. He gets heavier and heavier. I touch my victim. There's something alive inside him. Guilt flows between my legs.

When the blood is late in coming, I fear I'll birth the monster that gnaws at me, that clutches my innards. I don't stop bleeding, I can't sleep, I'm afraid I'll wake up dissolved into a stain. I keep smearing the walls with my ten red fingers. My body complies with its strict deadline, its obligation. I go out to the street to gather my scattered parts. I hide the bandages that heal my periodic wound. I lose weight, get weak. The contraband poultices thrown in the rubbish bin at the back of the yard. I try to retain the flow so I can keep existing. And so Dad will love me again, so he won't be angry with me anymore. So he'll stop looking at me suspiciously and meet my gaze again.

He avoids me during those days. But his eloquent silence transmits his message. *I don't want any blood in this house.* My body doesn't listen. It continues to erode. This is why I didn't want to grow up, why I wanted to stop at age nine. I feel bad, afraid of the lurking haemorrhage. Then the date comes, and the spring bubbles up from my body for no reason, weighing me down with the anguish of another time. And his fist bounces off the dining room tablecloth.

'I don't want any blood in this house,' he says.

I lower my head, fold my hands in my lap and look at the floor. I close my legs, suck in my stomach, take a deep breath. The bodies covered in newspaper. I bend my knees, open my lips, stretch out my neck. People leaving on a one-way train. I shrug my shoulders, bend my elbows, stretch my arms. A list of names is written out; a shovel scrapes the ground. I know that when I bleed Dad thinks, suspects, is certain, that I'm somehow related to that officer with his arm raised.

8

Mum Stands Up to Receive
Bad News

Ever since I was born, Mum has been dying. Her lips go numb when she tries to talk to me. But every time she raises her voice she leaves a wound. She leans against the walls as she walks through the house, constantly overcome by fits of coughing. For Mum, words are insufficient, which is why she resorts to more exaggerated expressions: opening her unblinking eyes wide, wringing her hands. The verbs crosshatching her body are written in a calligraphy that only she can read.

Mum is riddled with unexplained illnesses. She is the author of her inflamed nodules; she inscribes misfortune onto her body. Mum sweeps, leaving dust piles in the corners. She rests her face against the broom handle and thinks. She doesn't know about the nine-year-old boy who lives inside Dad. She also doesn't notice the home economics that we all practise: the apples we divvy up, the shampoo we use in tiny dollops, the litres of water we drink to quell our hunger, the extra hours we sleep to avoid spending money on anything. She buys new pairs of shoes, long dresses, throws out leftovers. She drinks alcohol in secret behind closed doors. I flee her vinegary kisses. She peers into the edge of the mirror to line her eyes with a dull brown pencil. She paints her mouth with the red lipstick she inherited from her mother. She turns over the photos in her bedroom, leaving only the image of a person who left so long ago she can't even remember when. My brother and sister's features float vaguely in his face.

Mum gets sick whenever she's sad. She lies down all day, her skin turning ashy. *I'm thirsty*, she says to me. I listen from the bedroom doorway. Her outstretched arm holds a glass of thick liquid that has sat on her bedside table for days. Her moans are raspy and she covers her mouth with a wrinkled handkerchief. She reads knitting manuals and practises new stitches. I bring her watered-down wine. And I look at her deformed creations: a neckless sweater, a too-short scarf, a four-fingered glove. She smiles weakly and finishes a backstitch. But Mum is a strong person; she always stands up to receive bad news.

One day we came home from school to find a sign on the front of the house with large red lettering: AUCTION. Mum was waiting for us at the door. Adela went pale and almost fainted. Davor went pink with rage and punched the wall. I wanted to run away: I looked down the street but my legs didn't react. We rushed to protect our plastic toys from the auction, which didn't differentiate between wooden spoons, sheer curtains, rubber balls, Persian rugs, beach pails, soup pots, mahogany furniture, china place settings, Lego pieces.

Strangers were taking stock of the house, the furniture, the decorations. They haggled, asked questions. They moved through our rooms with irritating nonchalance. They examined the closets, the cracks in the walls, and whispered amongst themselves. First they rolled up the living room rug, our wrestling mat. Then a fat lady who could barely fit through the door recklessly emptied Adela's desk. She threw out notebooks, loose pencils, cropped photos. My sister picked everything up without looking at the woman and stuffed it into her gym bag. A boy the same age as Davor took his sticker-speckled wooden trunk. Each transfer depicted a different country; he'd collected 107 of them. Now it was my turn. A young man was slowly looking over my things. He chose my doll Patricia. Shaking her cloth arms, he said he was certain his nine-year-old daughter was going to love it.

We spent that day hunched in a corner of the living room, in front of the television. Pretending not to care about the awkwardness of the estate sale. We were watching a show about the human body. We'd already learned how the nervous system and the respiratory system functioned, how the signals were sent from the brain. Now they were moving to the heart. A man asked about the TV set. Mum got excited and said *yes, of course, it's still under warranty, look how big it is, practically a movie screen.* She presented the merits of the appliance, gesticulating with open palms, like someone explaining a work of art. Mum turned the knob and the heartbeats stopped. She unplugged the TV set and brushed off the dust as the man signed a check. He took the set in his arms and left without saying goodbye. The three of us stayed frozen in place, staring at the wall, left guessing about the end of the programme. Wondering how the last organ worked: the heart. In the background we heard the squealing of the pipes.

9

Equations With Different Solutions

The day of the big maths test has arrived. The sheet lies on my desk. I'm paralysed, staring at numbers and symbols that have lost all meaning. The formulas blur together. They make me dizzy. Everyone takes out their pencils and starts to write. My racing heartbeat makes the images tremble on the photocopied hand-out.

To distract myself, I write *Maths Test*. I erase it and write *Exercises*, which I also erase. I write my name, the date, I look around. My classmates' pencils are flying across their papers. A viscous fatigue courses through my body. My palms sweat, the lead smears. I see black stains on my test sheet, between the operations, on the wiped-clean blackboard. I breathe deeply, my temples pound, my head aches. I try to look at a neighbour's test for some clue to guide me. I have an idea. I write numbers and symbols. I change my mind and start to erase them; the eraser breaks into tiny pieces on the page. I try out other equations and reach new answers. I glance around: I see only stains, mute images. I look back at my test. The numbers remain silent and static. I try to calm myself, but I'm terrified by the teacher's white smock, the state-school teacher's uniform that mirrored my own.

Floating up off the page, blinking like a mirage, is a familiar number. The two beside the four, the five and the seven. A painful number, the number of days the war lasted, the tears Dad has cried. The two thousand four hundred and fifty-seven days Dad is owed. I don't want that figure to rise up from the background of the page, ringing with my history. Or, if there's a three, followed by a four, a nine, three sevens and a zero it's the telephone number of the house with the palm trees. The number that the painter dialled. The man who slowly stole my mum; half an hour at a time, two hours, three hours, then four, an entire night. And the number three on its own is the triad of foods in the fridge. And if I add three and eleven, it's the fourteen cans left in Dad's childhood cellar. If I add twenty-nine plus seventy-five I get the 104 stickers on Davor's auctioned-off trunk. Three times three makes Dad's eternal nine years. I look at the clock. Class is almost over. I count the nine buttons on the teacher's smock.

The bell rings for break. The other kids stand to turn in their papers and I stay seated at my desk, blank test before me. Next time I'll study harder, I say. Or maybe I'll tell the teacher the truth: *It's not that I didn't study. It's just that the numbers mix with my memories and give other answers.* I stand, the desk creaks, the soles of my shoes squeak on the floor. There are no other kids in the classroom. I push in my chair and begin to walk. The teacher holds out his hand to receive the empty page, the reflection of my mind. My test crowns the tower of papers piled up on his desk. I mumble an embarrassed *goodbye* and leave the classroom.

I'm scratching a random shape into the sand with the toes of my shoes when the imposing white-smocked figure passes by. A ball of fire rises in my abdomen. He walks in long strides down the hallway, stops, straightens his glasses and continues. *You have to understand, it's not about knowing or not knowing, studying or not studying. My equations, my algebraic operations, have different solutions.* He has his right hand stuffed in his pocket; with the other, he grips his briefcase full of test papers.

10

The House on the
Palm-Lined Avenue

The removal van is once again parked outside our house. The engine starts. We move around the city for several months with light luggage. We have fewer and fewer belongings. We've already sold the furniture, the rugs, the appliances. I think back to the last image we saw on the TV set. The blood circulating through the veins and half of the aorta. Bambambam. The interrupted heartbeat. Our little heart attack. The lorry honks. I keep a photo from that steadier time. Dad and Mum hugging each other with the garden in the background, us kids piled up at their feet in our best clothes. My thick-paged notebook still has a place in my suitcase. We shuffle our feet in a circular migration that later shifts into a spiral. Suddenly we've spread out; my brother and sister live with an aunt and I hardly see them. Mum and I share the guest room at a friend's house. I don't know where Dad sleeps but he visits us every morning. A few months later we're back together again in a big old house.

This house smells different from the other ones we've lived in. The façade is dirty, but I like the iron bars twisted to look like vines covering the windows. There are stains on the walls inside, the floor feels like it's made of ice, the dark hallways grow longer as you walk. My brother and sister and I race through the labyrinth of rooms as our footsteps echo off the high ceilings. We run up and down the wide stairway to choose our bedrooms. The house is in an older and noisier neighbourhood, but our street is a wide avenue lined with palms. The buses honk as they pass outside, the pavements are scattered with potholes and exposed tree roots. Beside the front door is a large rubbish bin that we roll down the pavement.

On Mum's orders, we go out looking for furniture and decorations. We check the skips filled with iron bars, pieces of wood, pilled blankets. We find a chair in perfect condition, a landscape painting, a table with three legs, a stained pillow. We return home with our trophies and Mum is happy. She's waiting for us with a delicious snack: chocolate milk and sweet rolls. On another day's hunt, we find a pot, a rug, a stool for the kitchen. I find a crystal vase with a chipped rim. Dad carefully restores each object.

One morning I find her singing in the kitchen. I ask where Dad is and she tells me he's gone to his new job. I look at the table and see a bouquet of flowers in the polished vase. Its scar is hidden for now. I search for the secret crack in the surface: it's more visible on the inside, like the wounds I carry with me. Like the sutures on my maps, the marks left by history. Mum announces that next week a workman will be coming to paint and fix up the house.

11

Mum's Screams

When Mum comes home, she barges in with her towering height, her cold electric halo. My brother and sister and I freeze when we hear how hard she presses the doorbell. She darkens the threshold, then the hall, the living room. We retreat, walking backwards, our eyes squinting upward. One step and another, in reverse, holding hands to form a triangle with trembling sides. She lifts her shoulders, bends her elbows, and her hands are like a pair of pliers that close in on us. We're still clutching each other when she finally starts to croon a sweet melody. Then she hugs us, saying we're a trio of sad shadows. That she missed us so much. Then she quickly leaves us and continues on to her bedroom.

Mum and I stand in front of the mirror. She looks at me strangely. There's a vast distance stretching out between us. We search each other's faces for similarities and find none. But our smiles are the same. Her ever-changing expressions converge in my fearless pupils. Mum penetrates the mirror with her gaze. She's pretty. Her terse face, her chiselled features. Her enormous eyes sprout long curved eyelashes. She has a beauty mark on her left cheek. Her high cheekbones make her seem majestic. Her mouth a pair of wide and well-drawn lips. My eyes rest on my pale, almost transparent image. My skin is so white that

I can see inside my body. I light myself up with a torch. The beam illuminates the scars that time has erased on the outside and the stitches left on the inside. Mum forces me to modify my life story. To edit it. In her state of constant convalescence, I've begun to invent my own unclassifiable illness. Every month, strange ulcers pierce the inside of my mouth. My gums crack, my tongue writhes. The doctors can't find the cure nor the cause of this affliction. The tests focus on my mysterious bleeding. I stay silent for several days, lost in my labyrinths. My gums bleed.

We're in the living room. Mum turns on the record player and invites me to dance. She pulls me close; I reach the height of her breasts. I can't stop smelling the scent of milk. The music is a melody I've always heard, and she sings the words in another language. Mum insists we intertwine our bodies. We move through the room in quick double steps, humming along. Mum pants like a dog in my ear. We twirl over the waxed floor. Mum whispers secrets to me. *It's been a long time since your dad touched me. He goes out with other women. He has a lot of lady friends.* I want this scene to end. But when the music stops, she falls silent and takes me in her arms. She's carrying me towards the bedroom when my father enters with a present in his hands. She shouts at him. I fall to the floor. I look up and cover my mouth so I won't hear my own screams.

Mum screams a lot, and when she screams, she's not Mum. She shrieks like a newborn baby, an old person, a lunatic. She's reduced to the oval of her mouth, a zero. Her beauty, her exotic features, are summed up in lines and angles. It's hard for me to recognise her with her face possessed by this other identity. Her scream disfigures the set design. Her screams return her to her origin: she is Jane Doe. Her howl penetrates our small bodies. Her wordless expression courses in waves over the curtains, the rugs, the wallpaper.

12

Warped Dates

It's my parents' wedding anniversary. Mum refuses to open the present Dad has bought her. I lock myself in my room and turn the music up loud so I won't hear the shouting that reverberates through the house. The shouting absorbed by the walls, the beams, the windows. We all want this day to end. We're unable to face each other at the table. Everyone eats in their room or is mysteriously absent. I know that tonight, once again, I'll hear races in the dark, slammed doors, drawers opening and closing. In the morning, we won't see any crumpled wrapping paper, just broken dishes and a wine stain on the rug. On that date, Mum's shouting starts and ends the day.

I feel our lives filling with warped dates, incidents we all regret having experienced. We're trapped in the contradiction between wanting to be apart and not being able to separate. When Mum gets angry at me she says I'm just like Dad, that we're exactly the same, that marrying him has been her greatest misfortune. I don't know what to say. It's her against Dad and me; we form two separate factions. I notice that she looks at him with distrust, with rage in her eyes, with her nostrils flared. She insists we're both useless, good-for-nothings, disasters. She grabs my hair and pulls at the tangles. She shakes me by my sailor suit until the sleeves are deformed. She tells me again and again that I'm hopeless. I can't stand it anymore, I break down in tears. Hoarse sounds erupt from my throat.

Someone rings the doorbell. It's Mum's friends over for tea. She stuffs wet cotton balls in my mouth to muffle my tantrum. They quiet my sobs. The house looks so different. Sandwiches and loose tea set out on the table. The women come in talking loudly, greeting us with feigned euphoria. Mum, perfectly cheerful, shows them the kitchen, the terrace, her bedroom. I hear voices praising this state of obvious disrepair. Then they sit down for tea, served on the old and incomplete set of family china. I rest my head against the wall and spend the afternoon listening to the women's laughter as they swap recipes and talk about men. They're describing someone I know. *Yes, he's a good painter. He's dark, broad-shouldered. No, he works cheap. He whistles while he paints. He has very dark eyes. He's polite, he says excuse me every time he enters a room. He smokes at the end of the day. He looks like he drinks. He takes a nap in the yard with his shirt off.*

That night my parents talk for a long time. No shouting, just talking. I hear their incessant murmur through the walls almost until dawn. I try to make out a word, any small clue to the conversation. Nothing, just monotonous whispering. Sometimes it's Mum's high-pitched voice presenting long arguments. Other times, it's Dad's staccato pronunciation in short, stern lines. There are lagoons of silence, exhausted sighs, the rattle of drawers. I can't make out what they're saying, but I know that something important is going to happen. Another warped date that will alter the rest of the calendar.

13

Mum Smiles Differently

The first floor is almost painted. It's an ochre colour with white trim. It'll be time to varnish the bedroom doors next week. The house smells different; it's the paint thinner that lingers despite the open windows. The newspaper covering the floor has smeared letters, folded corners. I find Mum watching the workman as he plasters the stairs with his back to her.

Mum, watch out for that workman, I don't like him, he smells strange. Don't let him polish your eyes with his sandpaper or stab you with his drill. I don't like how he hugs me from behind and whispers *Hello my little girl* when he walks into the house without saying excuse me. Not like before, when he painted the kitchen walls and said excuse me every time he entered a room. The workman has dark eyes. I tell him we're different species. I annoy him with my blue Siamese cat pupils. His primitive eyes pause on Mum's cleavage, her sinuous hips. Lorenzo knows how to look and he knows how to paint but he doesn't know how to write a single word. He barely speaks. He wears denim overalls splattered with little stains. He naps in his cart, with his cloth hat covering his face. He listens to a battery-powered radio that takes a long time to pick up a signal. He drinks water from an enamel cup with a chipped edge. He smokes a cigarette in the yard at the end of the day. Then he changes his dirty uniform for the pretty shirts that Mum gives him. He asks for the day's pay with his hair wet and slicked back. *Madame, darling, my dear, that'll be seven thousand. Lend me a sheet of newspaper to wrap up the saw, I don't want to kill anyone on the bus.* Mum walks him to the door, they exchange a few words; I watch him trudge towards the bus stop.

She gets into bed without underwear and falls asleep before Dad comes home. They no longer speak. Mum locks the bedroom door. I see Dad on his knees, picking the lock, spending the night on the sofa. A wound in my chest, bambambambam, my heart beats quickly, it gallops and gallops, beats out of control, rises into my mouth. The workman's taking my Mum away from me, little by little: stealing her by the half hour, two hours, three and four, an entire night. His hairy arm gliding up and down the wall. Suddenly the paintbrush rests alone for a long time on the edge of the paint can. Through the keyhole I see them rocking on the bed, and even when I cover my ears, I hear the symmetrical squeak of the springs.

By the time the repairs are finished, Mum is gone. Her side of the closet is empty. Everything smells like latex paint and turpentine. Dad turns into a zombie, wandering the house in a robe with a three-day beard. Dad cloaked by the newspaper, hiding his fist of a heart behind it.

The heart that stopped mid-beat. Now Mum is a *Mum's visit*. She comes every once in a while and leaves me messages. I wait for her with my hair combed, in plaits, the way she likes. I shine my shoes. I wait half an hour, I stare out the door. The sun sets. She doesn't come. My hair is a mess, my shoes dulled. The next day she calls. *I couldn't make it. I'm so busy. Next week.* I hang up. I stare out the window.

Mum has to wash her hair with dish soap. Her hands are rough, her eyes sunken. She stops using eyeliner. She no longer shouts; it's been a long time since she was sick. Her expression has changed. She looks so tired. I give her a blouse I've bought with my allowance. She cries when I give it to her. She always wears the same outfit. She limps around in a pair of shoes with worn heels. Her majestic figure looks fragile, consumed, burned out. Now Mum smiles at me with a mouthful of chipped teeth and gold molars. She's far away, in another world. A new wrinkle creases her brow. And her gaze is different, empty; she hardly looks at me.

14

My Life in a Shopping Bag

Months later, Mum rings the doorbell and talks to Dad for a long time through the bars. They remain calm, distant, not shouting. I watch them through the sheer curtains. He comes in and I move away from the still-fluttering tulle. He says that Mum needs me, that I should go and live with her for a while. He gathers some of my clothes and my notebooks and puts them in a shopping bag. I leave in a daze. I can't look at Dad. They exchange polite goodbyes. I walk several blocks holding her hand, the shopping bag bouncing against my legs.

I'm reunited with my brother and sister. They share bunk beds in a narrow room. There's no more space, so I have to sleep with Mum. They send me to a new school. Now I go in the afternoon. It's dark when I get home after wandering the parks filled with rusted swing sets. I have to do my homework in the kitchen because Mum and a friend need to use our bedroom. When I hear the door creak open, I go upstairs and wait for the man to finish getting dressed as he curses Mum in the hallway. *Old bitch*, says the thin young man who has been coming to visit her for a while. He bounds down the stairs and slams the door as he leaves. I find my bed dishevelled, the room filled with a strong smell. Mum is in the bathroom taking off her makeup. I lie between the sheets, repulsed by the scent and temperature of that foreign body.

I can sense a new distance between my brother and sister and I. We keep opposite hours, which means our everyday encounters are limited. It's strange to be under the same roof again. I feel like an outsider here. Their spaces are clearly defined; mine is blurry. I know we should talk about that disastrous game of replacements and substitutions, confronting the other's image of us, serving the cruellest sentence we could imagine. But no one dares. The thread of tension is still pulled taut. I'd also like to ask Davor and Adela about the man who goes up to the second floor almost every night. But I don't mention him. When the doorbell rings around eight o'clock, they leave and I'm left alone. I make myself comfortable at the kitchen table with my notebooks open, waiting out the slow creep of time.

Now Dad has become the Sunday outing. He looks gaunter in his old suit as he waits for me at the edge of the yard. We spend the day walking aimlessly around the city. We have greasy food for lunch on a park bench. He falls asleep on the grass and I play with kids I don't know, friends improvised for the occasion. My shoes hurt my feet, swollen from so much walking. As soon as it gets dark I ask him to take me home. We say goodbye till next week; I don't want these outings to become a custom. And they don't, because Dad is transferred to another city. When he gives me the news I feel a mixture of relief and sadness. We agree that I'll go and stay with him during my school break. I look at the calendar. The months are blocks of endlessly repeated days. The date jotted down at the end of the year is a long way off. I mark it with a circle to have something to look forward to.

15

Journey in a Straightjacket

Mum looks at us from so high up, she smiles at us from so far away. She studies us without seeing us. We repeatedly catch her acting under the impulse of her trembling hands, tipping a jar of pills into her throat. We take the bottles out of the medicine cabinet. But she always screams loud enough that one of us reveals the hiding place.

The image fades to white the day we find Mum lying on the pavement, surrounded by shoes and voices, her hair damp and her eyes open wide. The long minutes of waiting after the emergency call. The ambulance siren, which sounds so different as it approaches our house, and the stretcher gliding over the pavement. The three of us hold hands in the doorway, watching as the vehicle drives away with our mother inside.

Mum in a coma, connected to tubes, in an old hospital room. Mum sleeping a long sleep, tied at the wrists and ankles. A journey to a distant place, with no luggage but a straightjacket. She is resurrected as we starve to death. She wakes in fits and starts and clumsily assembles herself into the here and now. She looks down at us from her high, rail-flanked bed, the starched sheets embroidered with the name of the hospital. Broken, re-gathered, and embellished moments converge in her new consciousness. Events accumulate under her eyelids. When she wakes, they take on a third dimension. We walk down the sterile hospital corridors until we reach room 503, the dark cave we have to enter. The woman lying in the bed isn't Mum. She looks just like her, but her face is swollen and deformed and she's fed through an intravenous tube. When they pull back the curtains, I see that her body is a sack of misshapen bones covered in cracked bluish skin. A paper bracelet with her name on it dances around her right wrist. Her cheeks are sunken, her eyes closed. The lines on the monitor, rising and falling with her heartbeats, are the only proof that she's alive.

After several days Mum murmurs something. I'm the only one with her. I watch her from the edge of the bed. I listen to her efforts, an incipient sentence. Finally, her voice emerges.

'Water... Adela...'.

'Mum... it's me, Tamara,' I tell her, as I bring a glass to her half-open lips and tilt the liquid in.

She stares, she doesn't recognise me, she drinks all the water in one long sip. Her eyes close, she falls back into sleep. I rush out of the room, desperate to find the nurse. For a moment I think that Mum has died. The doctor explains that she's getting better, but doesn't remember the last fifteen years. I don't figure in her memory; I've been pushed out of her mind.

16

I Don't Figure in Mum's Memory

Mum prepares breakfast for two kids every morning. She kisses Adela and Davor on the forehead as they leave the house. She makes two beds, fills the tub two times. She hugs one child with each arm. From the balcony her eyes follow two shapes as they walk away. She holds out one hand to cross the street, then the other. I'm left at the end of the line, clutching at my sister. She whispers a little secret to the right, another to the left. Her two legs guide two paths. Two tears roll down her face as she watches her children sleeping. She doesn't know the little girl who lies beside her and follows her around the house, snatching at her dress and repeating her name. She is incapable of including me in her twofold affection.

I don't want to hear her ask again: *Who's that girl lying there naked with her hair all tangled?* Mum never reaches my centre, just brushes around my edges, grazes my surface. I spread out before her like an incomprehensible atlas. A pair of steaming bowls are waiting for us when we get home from school. My brother and sister don't say anything, just silently serve a third portion on the bread plate. I have lunch at the corner of the table. And for a moment I want to drive it into my abdomen.

Another day my sister and brother and I all come home together and I stop to tie my shoes. As I reach the door, mere steps behind them, it slams in my face and I'm locked outside. I watch Mum, her welcoming smile, her wrist turning the key in the lock. Her world is a perfect triangle, not an awkward square. I'm the edge that doesn't fit into that geometric shape. For Mum I'm nothing more than an empty space in her brain, a black hole that swallows up all memory of me.

Little by little I'm left without any belongings. My toothbrush disappears, my pillow, my closet space. One day she gives away my jacket, saying it doesn't fit either one of her kids. My brother and sister don't say anything; they lend me their warm clothes, which I swim in. They try to hide her mistakes, creating a third serving of supper with strips of their chicken assembled into some unidentifiable part. Or they don't pull the plug on the second bath so I can have a turn as well. I submerge myself in the cloudy, tepid water, rest my arm on the gritty edge.

I decide to find Dad in the new city where he lives now. I gather my school supplies from the table. I pack my things into the same grocery bag that I carried into this house. I grip the handles. No one notices I'm leaving, dressed in my school uniform. I stand on tiptoes to look through the cyclops peephole; a lonely street awaits me. I start off on my first one-way trip.

ACT II

1

Permanently on Tour

The theatre empties out. My siblings, my companions on tour, act out their own dramas on other stages. Before I can put on a play with new characters, I wait for my next audience. The script is still being written. The plot, the characters and the stage directions remain unknown. I continue rehearsing my lines. I am deformed, mute, blind until the damaged parts come into view. My parents lean their backs against the wall, each immersed in a monologue as they wait for the end of the century.

The passage of time is an illusion, a frame enclosing a chronology of scars. I adopt the speech of my father, my father's father, my mother. Three human figures converge into one gigantic body, a three-headed dragon. Our eyes gaze across the expanse of wheat, as one dream follows on from another. A chain of loneliness. I see myself through others people's eyes, construct the outside world through the filter of my history. I divide the past into segments that return to the present like boomerangs. I leave all my projects unfinished, take off without a backward glance.

I stare at the landscape inside my eyes, delving into my own character. Shadows, symbols of abandonment, silhouettes pried open by light, legless men, women with stitches in their arms. The images swirl and merge into a stain that passes over the sky of my gaze. I close my eyes. My face floats in the mirror. I study the zits on my forehead, the pale blue veins under my skin. The contours and curves of my face. The shapes in my retina begin to blaze. I put my hand on the glass. I let out a shrill staccato sound.

In the mornings I copy the script of my dreams into a notebook with thick pages. Blurry characters speak and disappear, crossing paths without ever meeting in real life. They whisper messages in my ear, they chase me, they leave me. Sleepwalking, I cross a deserted terrain with my arms spread wide. I'm accosted by repetitive black and white images that fasten together like the links of history. They slide underground at dawn, only to re-emerge every night. A car parks in front of my house; there's no one inside, so I get in. My eyes are heavy and a translucent hood covers my face, blurring reality. Three lovers lie under the same sheets. The car reverses down my street in a straight line. The table is set, the women seated, waiting for men who never arrive. There are appointments marked on my calendar. I'm going somewhere, but I never arrive. Couples in unmade beds unable to have sex. A parched wasteland of electrocuted bodies, severed members, washbasins filled with blood.

I squint my eyes until I get used to the darkness, the shadows of the theatre. I pick up the flattened wolf hide that has been lying on the stage since the first act. I turn the heads of the stone statues. I recite my lines, I hear the cheers, I receive a standing ovation. Out in the audience I see faces I haven't seen for a long time. Adela sits cross-legged in the carpeted aisle. Davor rests his legs on the back of a seat. Near the exit I make out the workman's profile. Mum has her back to the stage. I admire her hair, her narrow shoulders. I get nervous, I forget my lines, the prompter whispers them to me. I look back and they've gone. I study the script. My character description: melancholic and distant; supporting actor. I don't know if I like her, but at least she's not the most unpleasant person in this drama, this tragedy, this comedy. We rehearse emotional dialogues. I don't speak with the other characters, but our bodies brush past each other, circle each other. My arm thrown across another back. Someone hugs my neck, kisses my toes, pokes me in the abdomen. We look distractedly past one another, engrossed in our own roles.

2

Sessions Between Four Walls

I talk about my mother. I've multiplied the two walls of the uterus by the four of my therapist's office. My choked voice rises from the depths of my seat. My prolonged silence lets me hear the whisper of the minute hand that only my therapist can see. The words gush forth, suspended in mid-air. I try to put together the puzzle of my past from the hollow of a moss-green sofa. One piece and then another, revealed in disconnected phrases, unfinished syllables, involuntary silences. She learns to read my expressions, my gaze, my tone of voice, my breakdowns. I hear my own speech as if from far away; my story becomes a monotonous prayer.

Twice a week, I put life on pause. My childhood starts to inhabit me, floods me with absence, leaves me little space to experience the present. Deleted scenes are constantly bursting forth: my mother and the gesture of her hand pushing me away. I cite words spoken by Mum as she put on her makeup in the mirror or swept the kitchen floor or when we danced in the living room. *It's been a long time since your dad touched me. He goes out with other women. He has a lot of lady friends.* I cover my ears as I sit on the bus and Mum's screams surge like an echo in my mind... *Go away, leave me alone, you're a tyrant.* I open a book and try to think about something else, but

I can't forget the phone call I shouldn't have heard. The deep voice telling Mum to meet him at nine in the usual place. I turn the page. I've returned to the summer before that, when Dad beat her legs with the TV antennae. I'm back in my present and glimpse the name of the street we're crossing. I get off at the next stop. I grip the rail. I have appointments scheduled, I'm late to meetings. My shadow always rushing towards a building, guided by the midday sun. I picture myself on crowded streets, locked in basements, underwater.

I can't stand that the therapist focuses on the same scene every time: me leaning against the window, counting the cars, while Mum is locked in the dining room with the workman. Her verdicts are painful. They rankle against my abandonment, against my misfortune. I leave dazed, without any sense of where I am. I walk aimlessly for hours. I begin to go blank at the start of the sessions. My mind is as empty as it was for the maths test. I'm swept up in the wake churned by the wheels of the neighbourhood kids' bikes. The spokes whirling so fast that they become a uniform metallic surface. My neighbour swaying to the rhythm of the pedals and her hair blowing in the wind. The aluminium rims sparkle. The laughter turns the corner. And it gets louder and louder, mocking me. I turn down that same road every Tuesday and Thursday. A streetlamp blinks on, turning everything white. I don't want to talk about anything else. I can't. I walk through the gate. I press the buzzer for the therapist's office.

In one of our sessions I tell her about Mum's illness and how she forgot me. I speak calmly, dragging my words through the past until they reach the scene in the hospital: her inability to remember my name, the doctor's diagnosis. I talk about the shadow I'd become for my mother. A ghost with no place at the table, no space in the closet. A silhouette hovering outside the door, locked out of the house. The nightmare of two of everything. The blind triangle – her, Adela, and Davor – which was really an amorphous square. I catch the therapist brushing her hand over the edge of her eyes. I keep talking as if I haven't noticed. I describe these events as if they'd happened yesterday, but many years have passed and I have yet to see Mum again.

I think: I have two mums. One contains my present – which is another form of the past – and determines what is to come. The other, a black hole, is sheer oblivion wandering deserted streets. I'd like to be born again with the therapist as my mother this time. I promise to be a good baby. I won't swim against the current, I'll fit my body to the curve of her abdomen, I won't tie the umbilical cord around my neck. I'll keep the waters of this ocean calm so that no one will get seasick. I'll stop the waves from rising up to her mouth. I'll sleep perpendicular to the tide. My little body will be a ship stranded in the abysmal depths. If you illuminate me, I'll be born under another star. If you lend me your womb, I'll choose a new nature. Let me be born again and I will be free. I won't require any special care, because I've walked here before: I know the rules, I know when it's night-time, where evil resides.

Then I go quiet, look at the clock, rise from the couch. The session is over.

3

Open Ocean

The screech of the seagulls and the murmur of the beach is etched on my eardrums. After I leave Mum's house, I live with Dad in a city by the sea. We have a small apartment inside a boarding house. The landlady washes our clothes and lets us use the telephone. We sleep with the light on. Dad says *Don't turn off the light or the black trees will get in*. One small burner serves for heating packets of soup. In the winter, the roof leaks and the floor is spread with pots and plastic containers. The electricity is often cut around the middle of the month, so I do my homework by candlelight. The black trees do get in through the window. We're always receiving urgent letters from the bill collectors about overdue payments. I have to fend them off when they show up unannounced or interrogate me by phone. I invent sudden trips for my father, overlooked messages.

One bill collector is different. I wait for him anxiously on payment due dates. He's thin and shifty-eyed; he wears a felt hat. Every time he comes, I try to stretch out the conversation. I spy on him nervously through the peephole. And I fix my hair before answering the door. I'm captivated by the way he opens his briefcase to take out the papers he wants me to sign. I always draw some random image, a heart, a star, a flower. He shakes his head and smiles. His cologne floats in the room for days after. Eventually, he fixes me with a different kind of look when I open the door. As always, I let him in.

'Would you like something to drink?'

I go to the kitchen and return with a full glass of wine.

'I bet you're tired, aren't you?'

He doesn't say anything, just brushes the shoulders of his jacket. He looks at me through the thin strip between the maroon liquid and the edge of the glass. Then he tilts the glass and takes a long drink in thick noisy gulps. I sit with my legs pressed together, staring at the floor, and start to wiggle my toes inside my shoes. He sets the glass on the table and wipes his mouth with the back of his hand. He grabs me by the waist and I smell his vinegary breath, then feel his rough hands moving up my legs. The wine spills onto the floor. He explores me with urgency, whispering words in my ear, making way for himself inside me. He hooks my heels over his shoulders. Suspended in mid-air from the impact. I press my tongue to the roof of my mouth, I don't say what I want to say. (Does he have to shake my hips so hard?) I close my eyes. I'm fifteen years old.

Dad teaches at the local university. He walks everywhere with his trouser cuffs unsewn. He returns in the evenings without noticing his zip is down. He spends long hours reading the newspaper. I lose myself in books, I have imaginary friends, I write endlessly in my thick journal. We're always hiding from something. I can't invite friends to the house or even tell them the address. After dark, we go out to walk along the beach, moving in silence for several blocks with our eyes fixed on the ground. I remember my birthdays with sadness. I often have to mention it to Dad before the day is over. There's never any money for a present. On that date I always miss my Mum and my brother and sister terribly. I hope in vain for a call or a card. I have just a couple of friends and I've invented a different life story for myself. My mother died after a long illness and my brother and sister live in another city with my grandma. And more lies. As many as necessary to hide the true story of my life.

One day Dad dusts off some old postcards written with smeared ink in small handwriting. He decorates his bedroom wall with these images of islands, stone cities, streets intersected by trams, a bell tower, an aqueduct. From then on, a summer sunset lights up the greyish wall of his bedroom day and night. Every night, when sleep finally wins out over the everyday drudgery, I know he walks the rainy turquoise-tiled plaza hanging opposite his bed.

The postcards are from his twin brother, a man I never knew existed. He still lives in their home country, on that other continent. He's a lawyer, but he works as the caretaker of a graveyard. He dreams of princes and eats a single meal a day. In the photos he looks just like Dad, only thinner. Every so often his postcards arrive, talking about people they know, distant relatives, the hardships facing their country. And he always charges Dad for vague expenses; all of his letters are peppered with dollar signs. Dad doesn't write back. But I notice his agitation whenever he gets word of his brother.

When I turn eighteen I receive my first letter from my uncle. He congratulates me on becoming an adult and encloses a log of family debts. I think about him and how, since he lives on an island, he must look out at the sea every evening, just like I do. In later letters he tells me that he lives in the shadows of the last century. That he speaks five languages. That he pays the rent for his small room with the tips the tourists leave him. That he gets kicked out no matter where he ends up. But that he doesn't mind as long as he doesn't have to go barefoot.

4

Circular Migrations

Dad is getting old. I can't stop it. I sense his advanced age and imminent decline when he starts watching the sitcoms he used to hate, slumped on the couch with the TV at full volume.

I want to force him to speak, to hide the newspaper he uses as a shield. I want to take it out of his hands, or turn off the TV, stand in front of him so he can't avoid me. To ask him if he's happy, if it still hurts that Mum left him for another man. If he misses his twin brother. Why there's so much bitterness between them. If he can tell me any of the secrets from his childhood. For example, what happened after the afternoon when the soldiers took his father away. Or when they notified them of his death. But I can't bring myself to rip off his mask. I'm afraid of what he'll say, afraid to confront the immensity of his pain.

Around that time I graduate from high school and move to a distant city to study at a place where I can combine my fondness for journals and reading. A place my parents would never lay eyes on. My blue journal, the site where I'd founded my homeland, now pushes me into new territories. For now, my ideas only reach the borders. The words don't yet coalesce in the characters I obsessively imagine walking blindly over the floorboards. I yearn to make them talk through their bodies and my own. I try to give voice to the stone statues and the flattened wolf hide from the first act.

I get a scholarship. I pack my journals, some books. I can still visit Dad once a month, measuring his deterioration in thirty-day increments. The morning before I leave, Dad asks me with a shaky voice to read him the newspaper aloud. I start with the front-page headline: 'Reformist Advance Following Election,' I look into his glassy eyes. I turn the page: 'Negative Balance for International Economy.' Dad begins to compose himself. He points to the bottom right. I read, 'Radical Protestants Boycott First Government Session.' My eyes wander the room and he keeps gathering his strength. I continue on the bottom left side: 'New Findings in the Oceano Case.' I look at him; he tells me to keep going. I read the weather forecast: 'Partly cloudy, low of thirteen degrees Celsius.' I want to skip a story, but he clenches his hand into a fist. He doesn't touch me, but I feel the blow. The font increases, turns to all caps, and I read: SOVEREIGNTY PACT FALTERS. TROOPS LINE UP AT BORDER. COUNTRY FALLS INTO CIVIL WAR. We remain silent. A new war is about to break out in his home country. Many ashes have already been scattered there. The century starts and ends in Dad's hometown. I know from the images in the news, the newspaper headlines, the breaking reports.

It's time to go. Dad hugs me and clutches my hand. Under the pressure of his grip, I remember that he was once a strong man. Without knowing it yet, I'm tracing a path of circular migrations. I periodically return to the city of my birth, the city of my youth, to everywhere I've stopped along my way. My character gets stronger. I count one, two, three, four. I know how to hold my breath. I stand up in the audience; I don't want to slump down and let things simply happen around me anymore. I walk onto my own stage.

5

Jumbled Shoes

On the first day of class, a man in a long coat gives me sidelong glances. He's average height, with an angular face, arched eyebrows. He hands me a folded piece of paper without a word. I open it to find images and a final line: *I have a hole in my chest*. I don't see him again for weeks. I find out his name from one of the other twelve students in the class. A dark-haired girl with long lashes knows him. Sofia asks me why I want to know. *Curiosity*. I spell out the word, concealing an obvious intention. She whispers the name in my ear: Franz. One day I spot him in the middle of the courtyard. He approaches me. Something pulls us together. The sun magnifies a cloud of insects above my feverish head. I have the urge to flee a certainty that falls like a curtain. His gaze is a charcoal line that sketches new thresholds, future desires. We share an identical yearning for loneliness. I want both for him to love me and not to love me, to call out to me and to forget me. This is it, this is how it feels; haven't I read about it countless times in books?

'Let's go into the shade, I don't feel well,' I say.

He follows as I guide him down the narrow path. We sit under a tree. His shape blocks the rays of sunlight peeking through the branches. He's a blurry body looming over me, cloaked in darkness. We talk all afternoon. His best friend Marcos joins us. He doesn't talk, just looks at me; I know he's sizing me up. Felipe and Jaime arrive. We talk about the books we have to read. Sofía smokes a cigarette with us and then leaves. Franz and I are left alone. He invites me to spiral down into his depths and search for blind spots. We are complicit in this silence that leaves things to chance. We study a scar on the tree trunk: two names. I run my fingers over the groove and my forearm teems with ants that he brushes away. When it turns chilly, he invites me back to his place. He makes me a cup of tea and drapes an enormous sweater over me. It feels like a straightjacket. But I succumb without protest to this man and his confusing limits. He is unable to narrate his past, to speak of people or places. He has very little furniture, just a chair beside the window. He sleeps with no curtains in a dishevelled bed. The day ends with a jumble of shoes next to the door.

He starts with my back.

His fingers slide roughly to my sacrum. He rubs his feet against mine. His firm flat body climbs me. His hands slip under my sweater, loosen the knots formed by too many hours of sitting in uneven desk chairs. I shift. His smoky hair falls into my half-open mouth. I'm dressed: his legs and arms trace mine over the blankets. Coating my lips with his saliva, he frees me from the covers and my clothes. He slowly unzips my skirt and counts my ribs. He caresses the sock-marks printed into my calves. I'm immobile and as weightless as the shadow he casts onto me. He stops me every time I try to touch him. Now he runs his tongue over my body, mines my navel. His torso dissolves, growing so distant it blends into the landscape of the room. My fists are clenched as he explores the socket of my mouth. His tongue sieves unrecognizable flavours. His body gives off a slight murmur, a decla-ration, when it presses against mine. I close my eyes. I know he'll see the signs of the things that have happened to me on my skin.

I break my stillness. A wave of sensation rocks me as I feel the contours of his muscles. The closer I hold him, the more he pulls away. The vibration of our bodies intensifies. Electricity courses through our veins like swollen blue threads. Shapes fold. A new form materialises and explodes onto the bed. We grow denser. My bones expand as I balance on the scaffolding we climb. I glimpse a hint of release and my arms strengthen to keep us from toppling. A fleeting death. I make out his outline. He lies on the pillow. I caress the curve of his skull and bring his head to my chest. My finger plays in the wetness of his mouth. I wipe it in his hair, its tobacco scent. I notice the curve of his back as he buries his nose in the perfume of my wrist. I wonder how such an amorphous body has been able to save me.

6

Minefields

Franz appears in my life and sticks around in a hazy sort of way. He brushes past me, lost in his loneliness. Other women, Sofia. I never let him come with me to visit Dad, even though I know he'll sleep with his sporadic lovers in my absence. A part of me doesn't want to let him into my life completely. I sense the instability his presence subjects me to. When I come back, he simulates order, feigns a need for me. He reads excerpts from his latest literary discoveries aloud. And no matter how often he empties the ashtray and throws out the cigarette butts, his apartment always smells of another tobacco.

'Tell me about your mother,' he says one day.

I take a moment to answer.

'Some other time,' I say, shaken.

'That's fine. Some other time,' he concludes.

That night and the following nights I have nightmares about Mum and Dad. I dream that my mother is fifty years old and pregnant. She comes into the living room with her enormous belly. I can immediately tell she's pregnant from the way she walks, her eyes. The ultrasound reveals that she's harbouring a three-headed monster with long ears. I open a door and my father is sitting on a toilet overflowing with shit. Whenever I turn a doorknob, I walk in on people in the same position. All with their heads down, slumped over a mound of their own excrement. In the next sequence I fill a suitcase with clothes, dolls, and letters. I burn it, watching the bonfire of my past. When it finally dies down, I desperately scour the ashes. My parents perform an abortion on me, claiming it's a healing ritual. They hold a green sheet over my body, but I know I'm not the one carrying a monster. I bleed and it congeals into little cubes of scarlet jelly. Secret codes whispered in a forgotten tongue. The messages of all my dreams shatter like glass inside my head. I fall incessantly down a long stairway, banging against each step. My knees are covered in bruises when I stand.

Several months later, I'm able to give Franz a vague and disjointed description of my mother. I'm skirting the border of a minefield. It's around the time we've started studying for final exams together, sleeping at his place. We spend hours looking out at the city from his attic room. The line of lights, the broken windows, the crooked chimneys. A group of men crossing the park. Couples kissing under the trees. Sofia always circling us, destabilising our precarious equilibrium with her long cigarettes. We wilt under her cloud of smoke, it envelops us, suffocates me; it trails us through classrooms, the library, the coffee shop in the afternoon. We're engulfed in one whirlwind after another: school, us, him, now me. I feel used up, adrift, my energies dispersed. And after every fight, he promises everything will change. And I hold out my arms to rest my head on his chest.

This man, beyond the despite-everythings, beyond the neverthelesses, is still a substance I need, but one that also fills me with distress. What I don't see coming is the new question he poses to me, waiting in bed one night with another woman. Sofia and her huge eyes calling to me, her long cigarette pointing towards the ceiling. The two of them awaiting my response. Then me, rushing to fill out the transfer form with the excuse of wanting to finish my last semester at the university's main campus; me, taking the train the next morning without much luggage, a box of books and journals. Once on the train, I realise I'm suddenly returning to the city of my childhood.

Outside the station I recognise the sounds of my early years, the flickering streetlamps. I wander for a long while, trying to find the familiar smells of exhaust fumes, mildewed basements, the pulse of the traffic, the buses honking like tugboats. I stop on a corner for a brief respite from the urban dance, the conveyor belt of faltering steps, anonymous shoes walking in different directions. On that corner, in that city, I can't stop thinking about Mum.

7

Mum Takes Me for a Walk

This is the street. Now I remember it. One day Mum takes me for a walk. We hold hands, it's night-time, we're coming home from the shops. We pass three women on a street corner. She gives them a sidelong glance, keeps walking, then turns back to face them. She says hello, they ask after Dad. Mum gives a vague response. We continue on our way.

'Who are they?' I ask.

'Friends of your father,' she answers through gritted teeth.

'What are their names?'

'I don't know.'

I can tell that my questions bother her. We cross the street. She puts on her sunglasses.

At home I draw the three women, the corner they stand on, the streetlamp that bathes them in light. I give them names: Trichi, Sussi, Virginia. I visit them in secret, make friends with them. They ask me about Mum, Dad, if they sleep together, what time he gets home, how many kids they have. I tell them it depends. In a way, there are three of us; in a way, I'm the only one. They laugh nervously. I show them my drawing of them. They like their pretend names. Trichi is the most fun. Her miniskirt rides up so high on her legs that her lace underwear peeks out. Her eyelids are covered in shiny powder. Her shoe is a stake that stabs the pavement. She chews a toothpick. Her sheer blouse shows her dark nipples. From her short wide neck hangs a stone heart, a gift from her daughter's father.

I start to dress like them. I try on provocative clothes, lipstick. I practise their bright smiles, their sinuous sashay. Hips swaying from left to right. But I loom over the spiked heels, wobbling from right to left. I feel embarrassed: first powerful, then fragile.

I seduce the dolls on the shelf. I beckon to the yellow stuffed bear and pick him up by his floppy ears. I give him a brief massage on his soft neck, move down his spineless back and pinch his tail. I simulate a passionate kiss. My mouth fills with fluff. I seize him roughly and force his amorphous arm to rest between my legs. *Come on, don't be afraid.* He stares unblinkingly. I caress the button of his nose. I try to open his sealed lips. *Why don't you relax, gorgeous.* I suck his ribs, the foreign tag with instructions for washing and care. I separate the two mounds of his legs. I make his mouse-like mouth brush my breasts. He slides from my naked torso. I pick him up when he falls onto the rug. I hold him up to eye level.

'Kiss me, little one. Stop staring at me with your stupid round eyes and touch me,' I say angrily.

I have to go to the bathroom.

'You're safe. The game's over, for now,' I mumble in his ear, then toss him hard against the wall. He bounces off the edge of the window. This time I don't help him up. Let him get dirty.

One evening Dad comes home nervous, sweaty. He sighs with relief when he finds out Mum's not home. He lies down on the sofa and smiles strangely. He turns on the TV but can't settle on any programme. He jabs again and again at the remote control. The images don't have time to load. I stare at his ear as he looks at the screen. There's a stain. I look closely. I recognise the purple lipstick.

'Trichi gave you a kiss, didn't she?' I ask, holding back laughter.

He stands up violently and slaps me. It's the first time in his life he's ever touched me. My cheek burns and swells. He runs to the mirror and rubs the lipstick from his earlobe with brusque movements. He says he's sorry. In a somewhat threatening tone, he asks me not to say anything to anyone. He places a wet towel on my face to cool it off. Then he rubs my hair and winks an eye at me. I don't say anything.

A car horn wakes me up. I pick up my suitcase and continue walking down the pavement. I decide to take a taxi. I look away when we reach the intersection. There are still three women on the corner.

8

Men Scattered in a Crowd

I stop and the images engulf me. Sofia's eyes, Franz's, mine. The cloud of tobacco smoke thickening the room. Sofia's blue skirt entwined with Franz's black pants on the back of the only chair in the apartment. The foamy secret. A three-year loneliness came after I left him. At first he wrote me successive letters asking me to come back. The minefield was now an empty map. I never responded.

Now, in the city of my childhood, I'm unable to reconstruct the memory of any man in his entirety. I move out of the way so that no one and nothing will even brush against me. I play the game with my own body or with other bodies. I go out running at night. Sometimes I catch the familiar scent of a man, but it's hard to remember; their images turn to smoke. I vow to never sleep with the same man more than once. Always at their houses or in hotel rooms. I sigh with relief when I hear the door shut behind me and the elevator creaking beyond it, once I've erased my nudity and emerged fully dressed in the doorway. If they ask for my phone number I give a fake one. When I get home I open the curtains to let the light develop the last victim's negative onto my body. I throw away a slip of paper with a name and address, I take a bath in the tub.

In these clumsy exits, I always leave traces of my presence: earrings, hair clips, belts, all intentionally forgotten. I imagine the pleasure it would give them to see, touch, smell these objects. On lonely nights they'll fall asleep with my things in their hands. And that will be all that's left of me, concrete and insignificant enough to sustain the perpetual mystery. Sometimes I wonder how I survive this solitary game. Only fragments of men exist in my memory. A random body in the dark at an uncertain hour. The night, the dawn, the room number, the morning silence, the final closing of the door behind me. I understand the dangers of those men in my territory. I sometimes think I see one of them on the street, in a café, outside a movie theatre, and I walk right past their questioning gaze.

It's New Year's Eve. I'm alone. I don't know how I got to this place full of people waiting for midnight. I'm wearing a silk blouse that glistens in the sparkling lights. I've always run from crowds. I keep to the edge of this party. From a corner of the apartment I observe the full ashtrays, the furniture pushed out of the way and the rugs rolled up. I force myself to follow the rhythm the others capture so freely as they move. It's a display of softness, scents, damp skin and cocktails.

Two couples sway on the makeshift dance floor. A dark-haired boy with a redheaded girl. A grey-haired man with a blonde woman. The closeness of their torsos is electrifying. The dark-haired boy whispers to his dance partner. She laughs, throwing her body backward. They turn, and the redheaded girl and the grey-haired man exchange glances. In synch with the music, she exposes her naked back to him. Then she pulls away from her current partner to show the grey-haired man her voluptuous bosom framed by red locks. The man, with a restrained smile, accepts the invitation. The redhead stretches out her hands, curves her fingers, twirls her wrists, drawing virtual caresses. He imagines himself twining his fingers in her thick red mane. She wets her lips, sends him a kiss through the air. The blonde woman shakes her hair, unaware of what's going on behind her back. Maybe she's noticed that her partner is embracing her more loosely. He has already lost all interest in the body adjacent to his: there's nothing more exciting than the other woman with her provocative stare, twirling beside them, wrapped around another man.

I lean against the wall. I take a sip of wine and watch. They start to plan their encounter. They play charades, miming figures over the shoulders of their partners. I look out the window, embarrassed. Another song begins. The grey-haired man pretends to whisper something to his partner, who trembles slightly. But in reality, he's spelling out a message that the redhead reads on his lips. They continue the choreography that interlaces their misplaced bodies to a pulsing beat. The music stops and each couple moves to a different corner. From across the room, the redheaded girl and the grey-haired man toast each other, raising their glasses and clinking the air. He raises an eyebrow, tilts his head in a *Let's go* that is both question and command. She considers her response, moving her brown eyes from side to side. Finally she nods the thick shadow of her eyelids. Both excuse themselves from their respective partners to go to the bathroom. The redheaded girl stands up first and rubs the dark-haired boy's shoulder. The man leaves a few prudent seconds later. The woman with the ash-blonde hair glances at her watch. He disappears down the hallway. I can just make out the redhead greeting someone. The bathroom door slams shut.

Someone takes a picture. The flash blinds me. I know that I was looking beyond the frame, underscoring my distance, my obvious loneliness. I play a secondary role, staying behind the scenes. I pretend that I need to fill my glass, just to have something to do. In the middle of the kitchen I spot Franz. I approach him silently. I circle him from behind, I recognise his smell, I caress his jacket without him noticing. I cover his eyes. He turns around and we're face to face. The first few minutes are a mutual interrogation while glasses clink and dirty plates pile up around us. Stringing our conversation together as the countdown to midnight begins.

I free myself from our embrace, I look around. I don't see the redheaded girl or the grey-haired man. But I do see the blonde woman still sunk into the same couch. The dark-haired boy is in front of me. He tilts his glass, stares for a moment, then sighs, blowing a lock of hair off his forehead. Both anxiously travel the perimeter of the room with their eyes. I think about how they'll have to unravel the designs of this new year that has just begun. I leave the party with Franz. The night is cool and lit with fireworks. This time I memorise him until I can spell his name on every centimetre of my skin.

Dripping from the shower, he lies down on top of me. I'm immersed in his coldness. Then I'm the one on top of him. My legs around his hips. His arms against the mattress. The sheets dewy. I rub his nipples and he squirms. He smells like soap. His temples pulse. His panting floods his ears with blood. I knock lightly on his chest, there's an echo. I bury myself into his wet hair plastered against the pillow. And after so much galloping he succumbs to his own desire. A salty stain on my belly. Franz's body is a familiar map, creased in the same places, but it never fully unfolds. I gather my nerve to cross the border.

9

A Hole in My Chest

That night I try to flee Franz's house. The dark room, my feet sinking into the wool rug. I feel my way to the chair where I remember leaving my clothes. I rescue the silk blouse before it falls to the floor. I look at him out of the corner of my eye; he's still asleep. I wet my lips, breathing slowly. I search for the sleeves, sheathe myself into the shirt. The almost imperceptible stitching grazes my skin. I close the buttons into their holes like little hungry mouths. I inhale the sweet and sour smell of Franz's sleep. It's dizzying. I rummage in the sheets until I find my cotton underwear. They caress my heels, my thighs, my belly as I pull them on.

I hear the roar of the first car crossing the street. I'm dressed as he sleeps naked; it's the first, the only thing that separates us now. I'm distracted by the tickle of his cat's fur as she circles my legs, prodding the back of my knee with the tip of her tail. A bitter taste lingers in my mouth. I imagine the kiss I'd like to leave on his rough cheek. I stop myself; it might wake him up. I leave the bedroom with my shoes in one hand and the other feeling its way along the cold wall. Reaching the doorway, I can't resist looking back. He's staring up at me, smiling. He calls out to me quietly. My shoes click against the wooden floor. I submerge myself in his warmth. I lie there, inside his parenthesis.

'Don't go... I have a hole in my chest...'.

He looks at me with glassy, begging eyes.

A hole in his chest, a deep well, a dry lagoon. I've lost all notion of my body's own limits as it melds with his, forming new shapes. We're a mountain, a plateau, a tree, a wild stallion, a star. We breathe deeply, gripping each other tightly, as if something were trying to separate us. During the night Franz whispers incoherent words, circular sounds in my ears. I'd completely forgotten about his protective thumb on my hip, slowly rubbing my crotch. I'd completely forgotten about his knee resting on my knee, feet pressed together, tired heads touching. I rest my head on the straight line of his shoulders. We stay underwater for a moment and then fall back to sleep together. I would have listened to you forever. You can't imagine the bewilderment, slipping into the flow of his thoughts. We start all over again. With his eyes still closed, his mouth sucking, biting, marking me.

I wake with his curly hair framing my face. We talk till dawn, plan outings, projects. We're excited about the idea of a trip, flying off together with no fixed destination. A journey through ourselves, but with another landscape in the background. We unfold a map and mark routes, cities, rivers. I can't fall back to sleep. The morning filters through the window; rays of light pleat the rug and sound creeps up from the street through the curtains.

Yes, that's what I need, what we need: a trip; soon, far, long. I look at the calendar. It's Tuesday.

10

Letters Exchanged

A letter on the table in the hallway. I check the sender. It's my sister. Her name, a strange address, another country. I don't know how she found me, but the concreteness of the envelope erases any doubt. I tremble as I unfold the carefully creased paper. It occurs to me that I could throw away the message and forget all about it. I lie in bed with the open letter and let myself be pulled along by my sister's perfectly symmetrical cursive.

Dear Tamara. It's you, Adela, I can't believe it. *This is the third time I've started to write this letter.* Maybe you're writing to give me bad news. *It's hard for me to write to you, just like I'm sure it's hard for you to read me now, but I want to hear from you.* Why did you take so long to write? *It's the dead of winter here. I have to stop and shake my hand to keep it from freezing as I write this.* It's summer here. I do the maths: if it's daytime here, it must be night-time there and you're probably sleeping as I read you. Your voice in my head sounds hoarse, distant.

So many things have happened to me since we last saw each other. I imagine to you as well. Getting married, moving here, having kids. I have a boyfriend and we're planning a trip. *I feel guilty about this distance, but Mum thwarted all my attempts to find you.* It doesn't matter, we have to make up for lost time, I want you to brush my hair like you used to. I remember the times I waited in vain on my birthday; the hope shattered by the postman carrying only bills. *Maybe I could have done more, but she insisted on forgetting all about you and your dad.* Tell me what you want. *What I want is for you to come and visit. I want you to meet my kids.* How many kids do you have. *You're going to be shocked to see how much the littlest one looks like you. I hope you'll come, I need to see you.* Me too. *Adela.* Tamara.

I sigh and stare blankly out the window framing the mountains. I reread the sparse sentences, so true to my sister's melancholic personality. I'm still holding the letter when Franz gets home. That day I tell him about a huge part of my life, though words seem insufficient. I tell him about my parents, my childhood, the real reason for the separation from my mother and my siblings. I also tell him about that first time at age fifteen. The bill collector between my legs, hanging off the edge of the sofa. Licking my body with his rough tongue, blowing hot air into my ears. The first time I couldn't. I remember my underwear tangled around my knees and him sitting on the sofa, annoyed. He returned the following week and I had to go through with it, because I wanted to, because I was afraid not to, because I was curious, proud. That second time he was more tender, he hummed songs, moved slowly; his hands, my dress, his trousers, my body, his torso, my breasts, his sex, my sex. Movements like puppetry. Before he left he kissed me on the forehead and placed the bill on the hall table.

The next week a different bill collector came. A thin young man wearing a cap with the bank logo. I asked him, with feigned disinterest, about the other man, and he answered vaguely that he'd asked to be transferred to another area. I ran to the bathroom. I looked at myself in the mirror and I saw that I was ugly, disgusting. My chin trembled, my eyes bulged, my cheeks were waxy. I hated myself for a few seconds. I'd never told anyone about it before. Franz listens to me. I know that in his silence he's connecting events. He looks at me from another perspective. The thundering sound of old worn-out prayers. A zigzagging knowledge of the other.

You can travel somewhere, from one place to another, inside someone. The journey takes the shape of an exit, an escape. We decided to take our trip sooner than we'd planned.

11

Dead en Route

We quit our jobs, give up our apartments, and sell all our furniture. We keep only maps, travel guides, a couple of suitcases. As we push the luggage cart up the ramp, tickets in hand, I ask myself what we're running from. It's the first time we've ever travelled together, together round the clock in a caravan of infinite days. The first destination: my sister's house.

We choose to travel by boat: a slow pace. Languidly crossing latitudes, long layovers, not mere pauses in transit. We want to savour the journey. The odyssey of our relationship is beginning; we've become nomadic. Taking off on an adventure with a one-way ticket, no return date. The ship sets sail, the dock becomes a tiny speck. Leaning against the rail, we assume our new roles as sailors.

We want to colonise countries inside ourselves. Unfold the naked map of our bodies and let the other explore our hidden, subterranean geography. The first stop is the reunion with my sister. A foggy morning. A silent embrace at the port. Our long conversations shine a light into the dark interior of my mind. Until then, it had always been a shadowy cave, scarred with drawings that future generations would uncover. I'm forced to verbalise so many things that had been petrified into silence. Together, we reminisce, holding back anger, sadness.

Long sessions sitting face to face, searching for explanations. The TV set sold off in the middle of a show. The principal notifying us of our unpaid enrolment fees. The workman walking through the house in his underwear. The sound of Mum's heels hammering away down the street. The wine stain on the carpet. The open bottles. The swallowed pills. Mum in the hospital, connected to tubes. The two place settings at the table, the two baths, the two goodnight kisses.

The memories rise up to form an empty temple, supported by columns that we walk through hand in hand. Sometimes one of us stops to circle a pillar, trying to decipher the message concealed in its grooves. Our footsteps echo across this vast expanse. Every so often I think the events I've so longed to forget are happening all over again: the night-time fights in the living room, moving from house to house, the auctioning off of our things, the workman, Mum in the hospital. Nothing has to be dredged up. We haven't forgotten a thing. We don't want to talk anymore. We go into her bedroom. We lie down on her red bedspread and turn on the TV. We find a horror movie, like the ones from our childhood. We laugh nervously. We grip each other tightly during the scary parts, jumbling the past and present, the two times occurring simultaneously. I look into her eyes. Her little girl's face is superimposed over her adult one. I see her first grey hairs like flakes of ash. She brushes a lock of hair from my forehead and rubs my cheek. Before, her hand was so big; now, her palms fit perfectly against mine. A crease appears on her forehead. When the credits roll I ask one last question.

'What about Davor?'

She takes a moment to answer.

'I hear from him sometimes. He's fine. He builds houses, designs buildings. He lives alone. He says women don't love him. Would you be surprised if I told you that you lived in the same city?' she said, avoiding my eyes.

'No. We hardly saw each other when we lived in the same house.'

She leaves the bedroom. I understand that she doesn't want to keep talking. I conjure the image of Davor in the blonde wig he'd wear to imitate me as I sucked on a strand of my hair and burst into tears.

Franz and my sister's husband looked on in wonder during our intense conversations. We're so focused on settling our past that I don't even notice my sister's present-day world. I leave with only a vague image of her husband. The profile of a man sitting on the couch, inhaling a pipe and exhaling smoke. I'm moved that her youngest daughter looks so much like me; it makes me feel closer to her. But her kids are most real to me in the vision of the backyard, scattered with toys. I know it's time to leave when I dream of the two of us dressed as brides and kissing in the back of a taxi. Someone asks if I'm all right – what a question – but I don't respond until I've opened and shut another door. I wake up. There's a feeling of something temporary, the atmosphere of a waiting room. It's time to move on; we have to finish our trip, not stop halfway. We're two owls trying to escape by night into the forest.

That morning, as I try to shake the image in my head, I talk to Franz.

'We need to continue on our way,' I say.

'When?' he asks, surprised.

'Today,' I declare.

My tone is so urgent that he starts packing without a word.

On the morning before we leave, Adela brushes my hair. She takes out my ponytail and combs from root to tip, separating strands, untangling knots. The light pull of her hands makes a humming sound. It's the sound of my childhood. She moves over the curve of my skull, following the line of my neck. Her light caress massages my head, creeps over my forehead. She's reached the ends when the phone rings. She leaves my hair spread neatly over my back.

We promise not to speak of the past anymore. I leave knowing little about her present: her family, her kids, her work as a translator. After this visit something inside me closes up and seals shut. The scars are fainter now.

12

I See Only Your Feet

Back on our voyage, Franz begins to feel like a stranger. I start to see evidence of the hole in his chest. That shadow he'd told me about early in our relationship: a tunnel that absorbs the light, the present, all presence. He takes long pauses, then resumes the conversation. We cross streets. We spend a lot of time together, but I do all the talking, never asking any questions. I think he must want an explanation from me. When he makes a comment, I can't hide the boredom that his opaqueness produces in me. He oscillates in the distance like a secondary character in my story. I feel like he's incapable of containing me. In our cabin, I start to undress with my back to him, to spend the night under the covers contemplating the ceaseless motion of the waves.

After the reunion with Adela I'm adrift on the sea of my childhood. I barely notice the changes of scenery, countries, climates. All the places blur together, it seems. In what's left of the trip, Franz never changes his clothes even once. It annoys me. The monotony is interrupted only by a glimmer of sunset on the window or a brief conversation with another passenger. One thing leads to another and a strip of land rises up to separate us. I can see the tunnel and us walking into it together.

After three months away, we still haven't docked. Our luggage arrives, our bodies, but our minds still wander some distant outpost. I don't know the exact location of the shipwreck; the storm comes out of nowhere, an infinite silence falls. Though we disembark on the same day, we arrive out of step. We're experiencing the exodus of our relationship. Our landscape fractured, a void opens up between us, and it's quickly flooded with our emotions and our shared history. Every stamp on our passports is a tiny obituary.

Now I only see your feet. You follow Dad's old trick of hiding behind the newspaper. When I come home I'm greeted only by your ankles on the table; the angle of your legs seems too obtuse. You keep reading without the slightest gesture of recognition. I don't know how to tear down the paper wall between us. I set my purse on the chair in the hallway and walk towards your bare feet, which rise up like another barricade. First I creep like a feline, brushing against the furniture, the dense rug absorbing my footsteps. My shoes trip on old resentments, distances and silences. I think about how our private story is being overwritten by public events. I stop. You remain impassive. I read the headline: *Teacher's Request Deemed Inappropriate*. I smile at the joke of the day. Then my voice leaps forth and I shatter the pregnant silence with my scathing words.

The sole of your foot is an unfamiliar map, marred by accidents, cataclysmic events. I peer over the paper with my right eye. I find the date in the corner that reminds me we've been together for three years. Your feet hit the ground, your face appears. The newspaper flutters gently to the floor. For a few seconds, we look at each other; the sentence is irrevocable.

13

A Conversation of Beginnings and Endings

When I wake up, he isn't there. I search the sheets for his pulse, feel around for his ribs, throw back the covers expecting to find his medium build. I sit staring at my own legs. Thoughts of all the other men I've known roll right off me, but I'm pierced with Franz's memory. I think about the abyss that extends from the edge of the bed. *Come back*, I tell him, pressing my lips against the window. I know I'll have to make space for him in my life. To hang a picture that might sum up our experiences together. To locate the exact point of our failure to connect on the map, root out the causes of so much neglect.

I have a sinking feeling inside me. I know that in the mornings to come I'll long for him to be there, sunk deep in my nudity. I imagine him surrounded by the morning's dusty silence, his eyes clouded with fog, his teeth grinding in his gums. The soldiers stand in the line of fire. He's gone: there's no trench to protect me from this surprise attack. I blink away the sparks. They strafe the centre of my heart. A hole in my chest. I stand in the middle of the battlefield.

Your words graze me once I've decided to stop listening. A jumble of sounds and pauses, moving lips. Your vocal chords vibrate. I laugh in your face, I cover my ears,

I look out the window. I choose words at random, give incoherent speeches. I read street signs and newspaper ads aloud. I recite commercial jingles. The sentences pile up on the blank page of my journal like moments frozen in time; doodles to pass the hours during this long wait. How can we merge our forked paths, how can we resist the force that pulls us apart, how can we establish some neutral ground where we might be able to meet again. It seems that change is no longer possible.

The last time I see Franz is in a café, where we meet for a conversation about beginnings and endings. The street noise, the waiter there to take our order, to serve the coffee. You light the first cigarette. We can't connect; I talk but you barely hear me. Other customers interrupt to ask for our empty chairs, the sugar, the time. The saucers, the spoon, the steam, the napkins that run out, an acquaintance says hello. I can't touch you: there's a table between us, two coffee cups, an ashtray. I want to say something but the waiter interrupts me with the bill. When I finally manage to look you in the eye I feel dizzy. Your pupils are a shale cliff, the line that marks the edge of the abyss.

14

Waking Nightmares

After I'm notified of Franz's death, my telephone rings for days and days in his empty room.

I don't know how to define our relationship: an unfinished conversation, an open ending. We'd spent hours in his attic room contemplating the neighbour's broken windows, the crooked chimneys, guessing at what might be going on in those lit-up rooms, talking about the endless surface of irregular roofs, loose shingles, antennas piercing the sky. Our walks through the park, watching the whirlwinds of litter and leaves, the builders with their toolboxes, our attempts to decode the footprints recorded in the gravel. Then the trip, the time beyond all chronology that we spent crossing borders, invading countries, sailing seas. Something changed.

The whistle of the gas pipes or your body swaying like a bundle strung from the ceiling on the old clothesline. Or maybe your wrists torn open and submerged in hot water. Porcelain and chrome splattered. I don't know how you did it – I never wanted to hear – but sleep comes after your final moment of consciousness. You open the valve and listen to the hum until you fall asleep. You trace a deep and precise line on your skin. You pull on the rope or slowly press the trigger, staining the tiles. I still ache for you in my sleep, when I see your dried-out toothbrush in the bathroom. My bones are dressed in worms. I close my fear-filled mouth. Lying on the curve of my lips is the certainty of having lost you for good. Your silent cry is lodged in my throat. It doesn't matter how it happened, but you close your eyes. You don't say goodbye. You're no longer here.

From the goodbye ritual I only remember the midday sun over our heads. The intense glare whitewashing the gravestones and gravel paths. I'll never forget the squeaky wheels of the cart that bears your body, its cries punctuating our shuffling steps as we follow you down the narrow road. I make way through the crowd of sweaty bodies and toss a handful of dirt on top of you to fill the hole in your chest, to block the tunnel we crossed together. I stand there for a few seconds, looking down at the grave as the earth swallows you up.

When I lift my eyes, your mother is staring at me. I think she must be silently wondering what it had been like to make love to her son. Behind her, the men dab their foreheads with handkerchiefs. I recognise the troubled faces of some of our former classmates. I even see Sofía at the edge of the crowd and I feel nothing. From so much pulling at my blouse, from so much holding onto myself, the fabric suddenly rips, with a horrifying sound. Someone puts an arm around me. I walk away, held upright by this firm and anonymous body, while you stay behind, farther away with every step. On the walk back, I build a pyre for all my memories of you. I keep only the last image: the two of us sitting at the table in the café. The fire devours places, situations, words. Sometimes wafts of ash still reach me.

Soon after that I go back to therapy. I talk a lot during every session, almost nonstop. I can't allow a single moment of silence; not like before, when I once sat for the entire fifty minutes without uttering a word. I talk about the trip, my past, my relationship with Franz, his death, the reunion with my sister, my estrangement from Mum. Often, the symbols are too hermetic to decipher. I start bringing my dream journal so I can read parts aloud. I uncover repressed secrets. I'm afraid that everything will come toppling down if I keep quiet. I leave these sessions feeling lost, distracted, my head full of blinding lights.

'Save yourself. Everything is sinking all around you.'

Those were the last words I heard.

15

Family Shipwreck

I dream of my parents. Dad walks along a beach, his shoes covered with excrement. Mum is a few paces behind him, wearing a frayed nylon slip. They get into a boat docked on the shore; they sail out to sea. The calm is suddenly broken by large waves that rise up from the surface of the water. The image fades to black. The next scene is the dawn of a catastrophe. Mum is the only survivor. Clinging to the wreckage, a piece of driftwood stops her from going under.

The next morning I run into Mum by chance on a street corner. Ten years have passed. I'm pained by her grey hair, her gaunt frame, so different from her once-voluptuous figure. She is no longer the film actress with wide hips, prominent bosom, long lashes. I'm now taller than she and it makes me uncomfortable to look down on her. She asks about me. If I am married, if I've got kids. I answer, shaking my head from side to side. She tells me she lives in a nursing home. I feel the urge to confront my long-dead past, to look it in the eye, to respond to that voice from the dining room announcing that supper's ready so the third little girl has to go home. She doesn't mention Dad.

That afternoon she moves her things into my spare room. She unpacks her suitcase, stopping to proudly show me a Mother's Day card I made when I was nine. My illegible handwriting and spelling mistakes are painful to see. I try to conjure that sweetness of red hearts and *I love you Mummy, Happy Mother's Day*. It's not me, it's someone else. I can't dredge up any warm feelings; there's only a stony cold. There's a strange connection between Mum and my recent dream. She's become frightened of water, has nightmares about rough waves. She can't even shower. She wets her hand in the sink and wipes the tiniest bit of water over herself for a minimal cleaning. Her hair is a tangled mess, and her skin has a layer of foul-smelling sebum. I wash her with a wet sponge as she trembles in my arms.

During Mum's long stints in bed, she spends her time knitting. I can tell when she's ravaged by tranquilisers, her energy completely drained. Her hands weave a series of complex knots that evoke her troubled past. Infinite strands of wool entwining into deformed creations: four-fingered gloves, sleeveless sweaters, too-short scarves. Her strange crafts are full of errors and correc-tions, fashioning irregular clothes that no one will ever wear. Her body recites its ailments. Mum speaks through her arthritic hands, crisscrossed scars, swollen glands. When I tell her about any misfortune of my own, she says that death is no accident, but the most deliberate act. Her death is foretold in the medicine bottles, the nightly sleeping pills, the wine bottles brought to her lips, the texture of the scars left by the passage of time. She can't stand getting old. She tries to erase the marks left on her face by so much screaming. She invests her meagre savings in beauty creams to halt her imminent deterioration.

Her mind remembers me lucidly; she doesn't seem to even register that she'd forgotten me for a while. Maybe I'm the one who no longer remembers her. She grows more silent, closing her eyes intermittently, suddenly remote. An older woman sitting at a reception desk. The ashen face of a rapidly aging parent. Our first conversation lasts two hours, we kiss and hug hello and goodbye, we have two cups of coffee, look into each other's eyes exactly twice. Who do you see when you look at me? This time we exchange three sentences. She tells me she can't stand Sundays.

16

Onstage Dialogue

Mum and I are alone on a wide stage. The floorboards creak with our footsteps. We enter from different sides. We stand facing each other some distance apart. We both clear our throats. We hold pieces of paper in our hands and we read from what's written there.

'Are you still going to love me when I turn sixty, my darling?'

(Pause).

'I don't know, we'll have to wait and see.'

Mum looks out at an invisible audience and points to the horizon of dark walls.

'Why don't you look me in the eye?' she says without moving.

'Because I'm scared you won't recognise me. I don't know if you see my double, my shadow. How did I return to your memory?'

'I don't really know. I put two halves together. There was a crack in the middle. I reconstructed you from a montage of photos. From the stories your brother and sister and other people told, until one day there you were, occupying a vertical space in my mind.'

'Reality is a negotiation. We add and subtract the past and the present. Do you have the courage to relive our story?'

'Yes, but the action should take place offstage,' she says.

'We can do it through a messenger, or a chorus. Or maybe a dream sequence, like in an epic tale,' I say sarcastically. 'You know what? Sometimes I thought you weren't really my mum.'

'Why?'

'Because when I was a little girl you never brushed my hair.'

Silence.

'Tell me, what's your character's motto, her favourite phrase?'

'In first person or third?'

'It doesn't matter.'

'I've made mistakes,' she says. 'What's yours?'

'I remember,' I say.

'What kind of logic drives you?'

'The logic of memory.'

'Now let's define our audience.'

'It doesn't matter. It's everyone, it's no one.'

I point to the empty seats. We stare down at our pages. My mother folds hers up and steps towards me.

'Give me a kiss,' she says sweetly and offers me her cheek.

I move away. Mum has a bitter and questioning expression. I shake my head.

'There are too many windows,' I say.

It's the first time in the scene that we look each other in the eye. The curtains take too long to close. Mum straightens her skirt, rearranges her blouse, absently pats her hair with her left hand. I shrug my shoulders, opening and closing my mouth, rehearsing vowels. We're exposed in our resentment, sustaining our desolate grimaces with the red curtain behind us.

17

Three Old Children

The tap in the bathroom sink has been dripping for days. The repetitive sound infiltrates dreams, thoughts, routines. The piercing rhythm punctuates our conversations, our silences. We're having breakfast. Mum knits under the table and suddenly an absurd, impulsive, inexplicable sentence leaves my throat.

'Why don't you call Lorenzo?' I ask.

Mum, mute, turns abruptly towards me. Her knitting needles clank to the floor. I can tell from the look in her eyes that she doesn't remember him. She has blocked him from her memory, along with the scandal it caused among the neighbours, their eight months together, his later death of pancreatitis, agonising thirsty and alone in a shared room at the public hospital. The rest of the day she wanders around silent and distant; she goes to bed early.

The next morning the doorbell rings. I look out the window. Through the iron bars of the door, I see the outlines of my brother and sister. They've received my message. I go into the bathroom to brush my hair and find the bottle of tranquilisers empty. I understand why Mum is still asleep. I'm nervous as I open the door. So many years have passed. Their faces are somewhat haggard, their bodies thicker. I haven't laid eyes on Davor in two decades: not a single photo or visit until now. His greying beard makes him look older than he is. His shoulders are rounded with exhaustion. I don't know if I should hug him. In a way he's really a stranger now crossing the threshold of my home. Adela has hung back and her warm hello reminds me of our special reunion a few years before. After we get reacquainted, I try to prepare them.

'Mum isn't well.'

They nod silently. They follow me down the hallway.

I don't know what she must have thought when the three of us appeared at the foot of her bed, how she could have configured the geometry of our heads bowed together but not touching. She begins to recognise us; her face takes on an unusual expression of tenderness. She tries to tidy her hair without much success.

'My three kids... you're so old,' she says with a thick tongue.

She holds out her arms, but they hang empty in the air. I feel the light brush of my brother and sister's bodies beside mine. Her gesture has made us all shiver. She picks her knitting needles back up and resumes her work. The scene is so absurd: the awkward and unmoving triad, the rag of yellow yarn no one will ever wear. Then an old image reappears. I recall the time the three of us held hands in the doorway, watching the ambulance take our mother away.

I return to the sombre bedroom, Davor's profile a few feet away. A ray of sunlight hits his cheek. I scan the dirty wallpaper. Farther away, two ghosts embrace. Adela sits beside Mum, showing her photos of her grandkids. She offers to take her to meet these kids with their almond-shaped eyes. Mum accepts, excitedly working her hollow cheeks, her toothless mouth reduced to a useless cavern. They spend the following days arranging tickets, papers, packing. The departure date arrives. They leave. Mum will send me updates on her illnesses by mail.

I face a new loneliness. People wander the city with their partners, their families, friends. I play at guessing what type of relationship connects them. I bump into other bodies. I crash against a jutting hipbone, a knee in motion. I walk in the opposite direction. I'm alone, moving against the current.

ACT III

1

Dress Rehearsal

My continent is this theatre without walls. It's this wide stage I pace distractedly. I look at the calendar. Only a few days until opening night. Each of us rehearses alone for the big show, when we'll put on the entire play for the first time. Noise from backstage. It's the murmur of the other cast members simultaneously reading their parts in their dressing rooms. The voices of my brother and sister mingle with the voice of my father, my mother, Franz, my uncle, a stranger, my own. The vowels and syllables stick in their throats and emerge in shrill, hoarse tones, floating up to the domed ceiling. The characters write each other's lines. My father takes the last sentence that Franz utters and begins his monologue. Franz repeats a word that came out of my mouth and links it to Adela's opening line. Everyone's secrets will be revealed.

Trapped between four walls, I go over the lines I've been given. I study my character's description. She never looks at the camera in pictures; she has the eyes of a ferret. She runs from her own shadow, her own footsteps. She belongs neither here nor there, which is why she has founded her homeland in a blue journal. She carries her things in suitcases or shopping bags. She's afraid of being mentioned in the newspaper and getting used by butchers to wrap meat. When she sleeps her long eyelashes point up to the ceiling. She waits for a phone call. The subway platforms switch around on her; the hours morph on the clock. She lives beyond time. She has the ability to be in places without being there, to inhabit spaces that don't exist. She's looking for a partner to learn tango. When someone asks her to get naked, she always leaves something on.

I'd like to forget it all. But each new experience breaks the seal and releases old memories. There's a certain exhilaration in an old story that disrupts the present. A rhythm that makes the past more painful. I'm afraid that the script will be too close to real life. My character requires me to be bolder than I am. Disguised by this other identity, I feel free, able to overcome my fears. I test limits I'd never even approach outside my role. And these unimaginable borders make me fear the end.

Together, all of us take a long dramatic pause, heavy with stage directions. Each person practises their gestures, adding more texture to their role. We analyse our personal dramas within the broader work. Different points of view sit side by side, each of us choosing what to keep or leave out of the scene. Subplots crisscross and connect before an invisible audience. Each actor pauses at a specific moment in their story. I pause on the trip with Franz, on our voyage by boat, our delayed arrival. On the hole in his chest that put him in a hole in the ground. My brother and sister pause on the death of their father. Adela is learning to write and she writes an essay for school called 'He's Gone'. Davor takes his first steps, stopping at a bedroom door. Dad pauses at the entrance to the cellar with the fourteen cans of food. My mother is frozen in the moment when she lost her two front teeth.

We move in concentric circles until we close up the holes we inhabit alone. In the room full of echoes, we try out our new voices, project them for the encore in which we recite the lines we've memorised. We wonder who will go off script. The path to the stage is a labyrinth. Each of us sets out from a different corner with a ball of yarn or spool of thread hooked to our belts, the thread continuously unwinding behind monotonous footsteps that trace the route. As we wait for opening night, we wander the maze, bumping against the walls. At each turn, we fear we may run into another person who will alter our course. Colourful threads mark the way back to the stage. After feeling lost for so many days, crossing open spaces and tunnels, we meet again onstage at the scheduled time.

2

Survivor's March

There's a roar of engines. A fleet of aeroplanes lands in the backyard. I peer out the window and see only dark green stains; I prefer to continue counting the flowers on my sheets. I stagger blindly in my circuitous escape. The mines explode, forcing me to run in multiple directions. The round summer sun makes shadows where the light thins. I study the featureless grief-stricken faces.

I walk down the sunny pavement. *Miss, can you spare some change please*. I hold out my hand to the beggar who watches me open-mouthed. I catch a whiff of his neck, the dampness of his nights wrapped in cardboard. A dog darts past me. I shout into his long ears and his owner, reading a book, is startled. Mum and her screams: I remember them, I hear them. They play on repeat in my ears. The recording is infinite, endlessly sustaining the same high note. A barrage of vowels, consonants, distorted lyrics thronging inside my head. I turn, I howl, sounds break down to form a primitive language. The raped woman, the hungry baby, the soldier wounded in battle, a man who fell from several floors up, my mother dancing with me in the living room. They all converge into one whimper, one distorted grimace, one oval-shaped mouth making a sound that is completely open and completely closed.

When Mum shouted she was a zero point, a newborn babe; she was not my mother. Her beauty was reduced to a few lines. Now her delayed scream disrupts my solitude, penetrates my adult body. It returns me to my origins. Her mute expression is cast over roads, intersections, stoplights. I try to escape her battle cry. I run through the city, but every space is contaminated by incessant clamour. Sometimes it's a shrill howl; others, a plaintive whine or a hoarse moan. My life is oblique. I walk diagonally every day to work. I can't stand to hear any jarring noise on the street – brakes squealing, a bus honking, a woman shouting – I start to shake, I have to cover my ears.

I glance sidelong at the newsstands, avoid the headlines. The current conflict in Dad's country is projected daily on his eighteen-inch screen. I'm in a constant state of mourning. I accompany him in his inner battle that mirrors the battle raging outside. Everything happens on two parallel stages. In Dad's country the bodies pile up to the sky. An identical nightmare plays out under his eyelids. The list of names pronounced through gritted teeth. I'd like to be a sniper like the one that haunts him. Before that, the advance of black boots evacuating homes. The advance of the trains towards the camps. The advance of the officers ordering executions. The advance of the gravediggers towards the pits. The advance of the planes bombing the villages. The advance of Dad and his mother hand in hand, escaping to a warless continent.

My advance is different. I advance in constant fear of being stopped. I get a new ID card once a year. I've just found one lost item when I lose something else. I like to look at myself through the window; a body lies across my bed. I advance through the city checking my dictionary. I advance through my labyrinth, lost, my shoelaces untied, my purse hanging open. I advance tirelessly, in a constant state of alert, practicing a march that Dad taught me years ago. And as I advance, someone covers my eyes.

.

3

Dad Is Nine Years Old Again

In Dad's country the corpses pile up to the sky. Dad watches another war on TV. He's nine years old again, despite his six decades. The lines of his face tense with each falling bomb. The fluorescent tubes of the screen replay the movie from his childhood: invisible gunshots, desolate street corners, people fleeing disoriented. He's an onlooker condemned to the immediacy of history. He feels a visceral connection to the events of his continent. He looks for the channel that replays his buried childhood anguish, which the rest of the world has only read about in encyclopaedias.

We watch his remote city through the fourth wall of the TV set. We see the broken glass on the floor of the war. The locals' terrified footfalls and the soldiers' determined boots crunch over this mosaic. Dad spends days in front of the screen, trying to make sure no detail escapes his knowledge. While I sleep, he stays up watching the live feed from the foreign channels, vaulting time zones, distances. He pounds the buttons of the remote control in search of the repeated images. When he has to leave the house, he records the conveyor belt of violent scenes. This time he's a spectator to the war that the main characters are enduring. The intermediary is the satellite dish, which transmits the image with a digital coldness.

Dad's twin is there on that other continent. His letters come less frequently during the war. They take months to arrive, and the envelopes have often been opened. The phone calls cut off after a faint *aló* that echoes in our minds. We rest easy because he lives on a remote island, where the explosions are heard in the distance. My epistolary relationship with him has broken off after countless refusals to make payments. My life slides quickly from one thing to the next. The only constant are my dreams, the shadows whispering words in another language. I dream of envelopes scrawled with cursive handwriting being passed through the bars, then the postman takes them back because I don't have the money to pay the bills. My hand still empty and outstretched.

We resume our places in front of the TV. The camera pans burning fields, boys' forearms with their blood type written out, kids looking back at us with a pain they don't understand. The shot widens and we're sucked into a dizzying sequence: blood splattered on the walls, halls lined with mattresses, a tooth encrusted in a wall. A journalist describes the recent events from the street where Dad once lived. His voice is carefully modulated as sounds of war play in the background. The camera frames the hills Dad explored on weekends. The camera zooms out. Now we see the front of Dad's old house, a window, a fluttering curtain.

That afternoon Dad watches as his childhood home is destroyed, thousands of miles from where he lives now. First the glass shatters from the windows he once leaned from to peer into the neighbour's yard. Seconds later, the camera tightens in as the last corner of the house collapses. The door he walked through so many times is blown off its hinges. The walls and windows, curtains and rugs are engulfed in flames. The fire takes stock of every item, every memory. The afternoons playing cards on the floor, the tram that passed under his balcony. The flames single out each moment. The snow that fell every winter, the conversation he heard from his hiding place below the stairs, huddling beside the fourteen cans of food in the cellar, watching from the rooftop as his father was dragged away. Dad takes a drink, closes his eyes and feels cold. He begins to sob. He's nine years old again and now I'm the mother hugging and rocking him in my arms.

'It's too cruel. Don't watch, let's stop up our ears, cover our eyes,' I say to him.

The same places are burnt again and again, caked with the dust of other corpses. Dad will stay at my house until it's over. I turn off the TV. The war is reduced to a black line that blinks for a second on the screen. I forbid Dad to turn it back on.

4

Address Book

I've met my university classmates for dinner. For ten years they've been nothing but names in my address book. Every time the door opens we try to guess who's arriving. The person can't see us from the doorway; they walk blindly across the restaurant until finally waving and coming over to our table. There's a moment of vertigo when we have to associate a new image with an old name.

I get there early, which is very unusual for me. I walk around the block a few times before going in. I've spent all afternoon trying on dresses, trousers and jackets. How do I want them to see me? Before leaving home I look in the hall mirror. I seem different. Closing the door, I slip my hand into my purse to touch the photo I always carry with me.

We're seated at a long table. The wine bottles block our view of each other's faces, whether unchanged or dramatically different. We exchange questions. We ask when. We ask why, which one, how many. We ask how. We ask where, what. I know it's all meant to determine who's made it the farthest so we can compare the results to our former expectations. The successes and failures of our peers weigh heavy on us. Over the course of the night, a range of ages shifts across our faces: the clumsiness of childhood, the pustules of adolescence, the hard expressions of early adulthood. They flicker in each person's expression like a crack of light beneath a closed door.

It's impossible to avoid talking about Franz, who obviously couldn't make it tonight. There will never again be twelve of us. Each person has their own interpretation of events. It makes them uncomfortable to talk about him in front of me. Everyone knew about our hermetic relationship. I know that his death triggers a different reaction in each person. Marcos, his best friend, feels guilty. Felipe experiences an unutterable relief; they were always competing. Sofía lights one cigarette after another; I know she still mourns him. I'm still jealous; I can hardly look at her. She hides behind her curls of smoke. Jamie is confused and sad; they didn't get along, but they were so similar. Mónica, Sandra and Paola, I know they're sad, too; they admired him, they loved him. Roberto is a mystery; he never expresses his feelings, and once again I have no idea what he's thinking. Analía seems resentful towards me, as if I should have been able to prevent his death.

The adult dinner takes on a juvenile tone, just like the old days in the classroom. Little by little we strip off our suit jackets and serious demeanours. True to form, Marcos takes the reins. He thrives on attention. He doesn't disappoint; we light him up. Alone, he's no one. He gets easy laughs, telling the same stories as always. Then he and Felipe begin to imitate our professors, now retired. The philology professor's limp, the shrill voice of the theory teacher. I mostly keep quiet. I talk to Sofía without looking at her. *Come on. Listen, Sofía, time keeps everything intact: the bitterness, the love, and the jealousy. If we could just look each other in the eyes, we'd put all our shared secrets to rest.* Someone laughs loudly. Someone covers their mouth with their hand. Someone coughs. Someone knocks over a glass. Someone moves a chair. Someone looks at their watch. Someone stands. Someone closes their eyes. Someone lights a cigarette. I don't remember who.

After the reunion, we'll be stuck for a while in that rewound time. We'll feel a tinge of loss until the rush of the present makes us pack our memories away. We begin to forget that night. One by one the names will be tucked back into the address book until the next reunion. We say goodbye, promising to call more often. I receive several long hugs that I read as delayed condolences.

I undress in the dark and notice the smell of tobacco on my clothes. Before going to bed I kiss Franz's black-and-white image. I repress his memory until he disappears in a gust of wind, obscured by some everyday occurrence. When I get too close to Franz he pushes me back into the world. I kill him inside me, murder his body inside my own. In the bodies of men with different names. I turn away from his mouth, release my hair from the grip of his hand. I rub away his fingerprints, tattooed on my back. I wipe his face from my retinas, erase the line he traced between my breasts. The sweat from his torso evaporates. Then the effect of the sleeping pills, blind eyes, my sex sealed shut.

5

The War Ended Last Night

The war ended last night. The spectacle we'd been witnessing onscreen is finally over. The war has ended, a reporter announces. Dad toasts with a glass of wine. The breaking news interrupts regularly scheduled programming, is repeated between movies, during the commercial breaks. A still image of the executioner with his arms held high under orders from his superior. And Dad opens the second bottle. There's nothing left standing: the city is in ruins. The officers writhe on the ground, succumb to panic attacks. The refugees plod along the roads of the new country that has been formed. They look down at their feet as they cross new borders. They move in fear of a surprise retaliation; their furtive glances try to distinguish allies from enemies. Dad's vision is blurred; he reads the label of his bottle aloud.

Dad makes a toast, tilting his last glass until it's empty, his eyes moist. He curses the generals as they file past. His tongue trips; he can no longer enunciate. He mumbles a nostalgic speech. He stares at the flag flying onscreen. Dad was born in a country that no longer exists. His nationality is a fantasy, his passport issued by a made-up republic. His homeland has been fragmented: different words for the same name. Below the streets, people stir from underground hiding places. The map he'd been able to draw from memory is now a random sketch. Dad is without a country, condemned to perpetual emigration. He opens his address book of crossed-out names. Each year there are more; each year he's more and more alone. He mumbles some names, he counts his living. I think about my own address book and the name I've had to erase.

That night, after watching another continent's news on TV all day long, I take Dad back to his place. He insists on driving. He's euphoric, unstable. I don't dare argue with him. All I remember are the parallel streets forming a continuous line of light; I see only shapes, trees racing past, yellow stripes. The roar of the engine, the clutch, third gear. Dad says something I can't understand in his garbled diction. Suddenly an intersection, a stoplight, a brightness that expands and pierces my eyes. A skidding sensation framed by chrome edges and a steel roof. Then a cluster of anonymous faces staring at us from the pavement. A voice over a radio describes a man crushed against a steering wheel. It's my father. The wind howls and rocks tumble down the street.

Dad's life fades out among blinking lights and twisted metal on the same day that the war in his country ends. He lies motionless, staring up at the roof of the car. An orange brightness filters through the haze and lights up a halo of suspended particles. Birds disperse in different directions. Conflicts raging on parallel stages converge, crushing me.

6

The Silence of Tragedy

A herd of horses crosses the orange horizon. Their hooves stir up fire and water. Their manes flutter in the wind. I hear the rhythmic sound of their gallop. Colts lean over my body as I lie on the slope of a deserted hill. I shrink away in fear. I can't move; the horses come closer. I try to lift my arms and cover my face. I can't. I remain immobile, glued to the ground, listening to their symmetrical hoofbeat. Suddenly darkness falls. Silence. The animals stampede over my anaesthetised body. I want to scream, but I barely manage to part my lips. Their hooves don't hurt; they're a mute, vague weight. I choke on the dust they kick up, I chew dirt, I cough. I try to swallow my saliva. My tongue runs across cracked gums. My legs are heavy; my arms are rocks falling into a well. A woman grabs me through a cloud of smoke before I plunge into the abyss. I struggle to open my eyes: it's the nurse injecting me with the first painkiller of the morning.

Regaining consciousness, I stare at the door of my hospital room, at all the thresholds I've ever crossed. I study the room, the white walls, the window that frames arid mountains. I look at the monitor and its zigzagging sketch of my vital signs. The back of my hand is pierced with tubes that crisscross my body, transporting viscous liquids. My palate tastes bitter, my mouth pooled with saliva. The doctor checks numbers, takes my temperature. He says I'm getting better.

'What about Dad?' I ask, fearful, already knowing the response.

The doctor shakes his head. I ask him to leave me alone and not to allow any visitors.

I remember the accident, the silence of the tragedy. The stillness of the demolished street corner and gnarled metal. The windshield was a mosaic, our shadows lying motionless on the other side, held in place by a fragile equilibrium. A ball of fire passed over us, leaving a trail of images in its wake. A universe of mute sirens and blind glass. I didn't know how much time had passed, or that I'd been taken by ambulance to the hospital, or about the goodbye I left unsaid.

The first thing I do when I get home is cover the mirrors with sheets and shut myself in the bathroom. I run my fingers over the sink, sit on the toilet, feel the smooth porcelain edges. There's no filth or fuzz or residue of excrement. Dad couldn't tolerate it. I flush, hypnotised by the rush of water. I go into the guest room as if stepping onto foreign soil. I check the drawers until I find his notebook with lists of food. I open the pantry. I rearrange the cans. I move the bags of rice, the jars, the sugar, the cartons of long-life milk. Then I lock away that chaos of packages and containers.

I find seven dusty newspapers in the hallway, their corners folded and the ink smudged. I pick up the stack of papers, read the headlines, the front pages. I think about Dad's daily routine. I open the Tuesday paper. The day of the accident. The top story gives no hint of what's to come. The second, from Wednesday, is as dirty as if it had been buried with Dad. The Thursday paper is white, the ink faded, the paper stiff. I spend the morning slowly turning the pages. I skip the obituaries. I devour the news in an attempt to recreate Dad's way of avoiding reality. But it's me avoiding the memory of him.

7

My Words Are a Scream on the Page

I flip through the pages of my family photo album. I always appear in the background. This writing is the manifestation of that exercise: I'm fascinated by the horror and sadness I describe. My words are a scream on the page. As I write about my life, I cease to be part of it. A new existence emerges from between the lines.

I'm back to my routines after seven days shut away inside, saying goodbye to Dad. I've spent half that time in the hospital. The outside world feels threatening. The noise of the city floods my ears: the roar of the traffic, the car horns, too many voices. The sunlight blinds me. The whirlwind of pedestrians makes me dizzy; my steps falter. I read signs and billboards as if I'd never seen them before. I feel like I'm in an unfamiliar place, where the inhabitants speak a language I don't understand.

I look at people like they're passengers on a different journey. I get on the last carriage of the train; no one else is going where I am. The pain has lessened and now only throbs in my legs. I empty myself of everything that happened, dragging forth memories I'm not sure are real. I want to spell out what has been silenced. My private words climb out of my journals. Dad's remote, metallic voice skitters off the walls. I'm shattered into a thousand pieces. My diaphragm is choked with rage. I walk over the hot pavement. I close my eyes to absorb the stammering voice of the city. I tie the immense crowd of anonymous beings into a single bundle.

I become one with the ceiling, hypnotised by the window and the horizon and the mountains. I kiss the glass, caress my reflected image. I'm the vehicle of past echoes in my memory. I see my face as a girl. I'm wearing the dress I got for my twelfth birthday. It catches fire: the pleats, the hem. Flames fill the pockets. The petticoat blazes, the lace, the buttons, the starched collar. And now I'm clothed in ashes, in shreds of flame-retardant material. I set out on a long march back to my ever-shifting roots. I walk through a door and don't know whether to go right or left. I listen for other voices to fill my thundering heart. Bambambam. I'm trapped inside my own existence. I'm uninhabited. The maps don't register my territory.

I think it's time to make the trip back. To stop travelling only in postcards on a greyish wall. To stop tracing the topography of illustrations and faded photographs. My character demands a new dramatic turn. I continue my march towards another continent of origins and separations.

8

A Trip to the Other Continent

Now that Dad is gone, I want to relive my loss in the asymmetrical image of his twin brother. I write to my uncle again, after years and years, to announce my arrival on his continent. To seek out Dad's brother is to jump into a bottomless well. To look for him in the negative of a photo, between the lines of his stories. I imagine how the conversation will go when we finally meet. I copy it down in my journal, I make it up all over again, I practise, looking at a picture of my dad folded in half.

My passport. My face when I was twenty, travelling with Franz. Driving down the highway with the landscape framed by the window. Mute landmarks, trees and bill boards with numbers succeed one another as I approach the airport. The sun slanting to the left of the highway. It's the reddest time of the afternoon. I've been writing about this trip for so many years; now I'll finally start to experience it. I hold the familiar postcards in my hands. I picture Dad and Franz in my head. I tick the boxes on the form. The voice on the loudspeaker announces the departure of my flight.

I've returned to my misty origins, the beginning of the end. I feel uncomfortable being a late witness to all this destruction. Walking the streets, I picture Dad as a child. I study the kids playing with their backs to me and I know I'm looking for that little nine-year-old boy, wanting to protect him from everything that will happen. I walk through parks and watch games improvised out of leftovers from the war. Inactive grenades are building blocks; castles are crowned with bullets. I take in their olive-skinned faces and pale eyes. I'd like to hug them, to shield their tiny bodies, to mitigate the damage done. I pull myself together, pick up my suitcase. I've come here to see things their eyes have already seen.

I want to visit this place before travelling to the island where Dad's twin lives. I make my way to a café on a quiet corner. It's the dead time of day on a summer afternoon. All faces turn toward me when I enter, sizing me up, especially the man with a prosthetic leg behind the counter. I ask him for something to drink. To speak to me, he takes his dentures from the pocket of his jacket and tucks them into his mouth. He must've lost weight in recent years; his clothes hang loose on his frame. Only his liver has grown dangerously large. The old people smile at me with red gums and glassy eyes. The kids melt ice cubes in their mouths. Leaning on the bar, I drink a soda and stare at the wall. Behind me, I feel the stories being knitted together by the characters of this forgotten corner of the world. By these people who have forgotten themselves. Everything foreign, like me, is a missing piece that might help them solve a new puzzle. I'm a foreigner, although my features allow me to fit in with them. I lift the glass to my lips. A small thread of sweat slides down my neck. I'm among the people I thought I belonged to. But I can feel the distance, the difference. I don't wear the war written on my face like they do.

A city where grass grows in the floors of the buildings, in the cracked concrete of the avenues.

9

Meeting My Other Dad

There's a boy. His skinny legs hang like sticks inside his trousers. I think he must be the last child left. The last child and there are no more. His fingernails are dirty. He's been playing war in the back yard. I ask him his name and his age. Erick. He holds up nine fingers.

I show him the slip of paper with my uncle's address on it. He points towards a corner I can see in the distance. The curve of the street gets ahead of me and blocks my path, interrupting my direct route. I walk through an arched hallway and stop to take in the rows of rectangles. A clock inside a tomb shows a forgotten time. I feel slightly claustrophobic inside this walled city. What will he be like? How much will he look like Dad? Despite my myopia, I see the silhouette of my dad's twin at the other end of the cemetery.

A warm embrace, an air kiss. I confuse him for Dad. I'm overwhelmed by the similarity. I stare at him for so long that he becomes uncomfortable. I finally notice the small differences I needed to see. I don't hear him when he asks me how my journey was. I'm split in half. I don't even register when he picks up my suitcase in a display of strength. I follow a few paces behind him. From the back it could easily be Dad. That rigid gait, the lowered head. But I know that if he turns around I'll see another man's face.

We have coffee on the terrace of his apartment. He lives alone. We're both nervous. After every sip we smile and look at the sea. He points out the tower from the postcards he sent. We hear the ringing of the bells. I study his collection of porcelain dogs. He talks to these dogs, which he ordered from a catalogue. He's named each and every one of them. The English Shepherd is named Jack. He takes them out for walks one at a time in his pockets. He glues their broken ears back on. It's getting late. We go into the living room. There are family pictures on the tables and shelves. In one of them, twin boys sit together on a chair. They're wearing short suits; both look stiff and uncomfortable. Another image shows my grandmother with a hat and a suitcase; there's a ship in the background. In the photo beside her, my grandfather poses in his military uniform. In the next, his older sister holds my dad as a baby. Then the three brothers are waving their hands. Below that, Dad is buried in snow, laughing. Then come the group photos of people at parties, on trips, saying goodbye in train stations. I admire these family photos. He responds rudely that they're no more than blood relations who write him a letter every once in a while.

I'd always thought I'd make this trip with Dad. I can picture him showing me around the place where he grew up. Taking me to see his school, the park where he played, the town centre. Now I stroll the streets with my other dad, his double, his rival. As we walk, I consider the irony of my uncle's profession: he guards tombs but must not even know where his own father is buried. A stone wall engraved with names rises up immensely in the middle of the main square, as if the height represented the number of absent bodies. The victims' final destination. Bambambam, bambambam, is the music of machine guns, a melody that can still be heard even though it's not playing. A beggar looks at himself in a shard of mirror. Maybe he's asking his own face to have mercy on him. He brushes what's left of his teeth. I study the names of the bodies scattered across this country that has been battered by constant wars. Among those names is my grandfather's. Bambambam, thunder the notes inside my heart.

I've been thinking about it for several hours. I finally speak up. *I need you to tell me about the death of your father, my grandfather. Dad could never talk about it.* He takes a deep breath, looks off into the distance. Now he speaks. In the middle of the night they knocked on the door. His mother told them to hide. A few seconds later, their mother's wails reached the cellar where the three boys were crouched in a corner, trembling, beside the cans of food. The fourteen cans trembling too. And with that sustained howl from their mother's throat, they knew the irrevocable truth. Afterwards, the selling off of all possessions – jewellery, rugs, paintings, clothes – so they could escape to a place without wars. His tone of voice changes. He warns me that he's going to tell me about something terrible that started out as a game.

The twins began stealing to help their mother. There was so much free time during the war, since schools and other places were all closed. The two boys roamed the town, taking belongings from the dead bodies lying in the streets. Gold rings, watches, pens, coins. They almost never looked at the faces, which were covered in newspaper. They went farther and farther into the outskirts because they weren't the only ones who did this kind of exploring. On one occasion my father took a pocket watch that looked familiar once they'd cleaned it up. It had Roman numerals, a grey face and a long silver chain topped off with a pair of initials. It was their father's watch. Tick-tock, tick-tock, tick-tock. Dad took off running and didn't speak for days. Tick. My uncle uncovered the body and saw the face that appeared in his dreams every night as he lay on his mattress. Tock. He'd heard at home that the dead had to be buried, not left out to suffer in the sun. Tick. He went back the next day. The street was empty. Tock.

When he finishes the story, I notice that my trousers are wet, my knees cold and my stomach bloated. Tick. I've begun to bleed. Tock. I clench my muscles but the lukewarm lava flows out. Tick. Once again my body complies with the order of its erosion. Tock. I don't want to be the bearer of blood linked to the death of my grand-father. Tick. I'm afraid my uncle will notice. Tock. Afraid that he too will suddenly pound the table and forbid blood in his home. Tick. I think about what would happen if I wrote his name and mine on the tiles with this fluid. Tock. Or if I were to smear this country with my ten red fingertips. Tick. He has already stolen from the dead; perhaps he'd like to suck my bloody fingers. Tock. But he might not be able to spit it out. Tick. I lower my head, clasp my hands in my lap and look at the floor. Tock.

I stand up and go outside for a long walk. I reach the empty train station. I go to the platform. There's one train carriage stopped there. I imagine that this is the station Dad dreamed about. I see the faces of the lost children, the vacant eyes of the women, the hunched backs of the men. There are hundreds, thousands of them, boarding the trains, I see them move away, their arms stretching from the narrow windows, gesturing wildly. I step onto the track, look at the solitary carriage. I watch until the darkness of a tunnel swallows the last shapes and the locomotive smoke disappears. I begin to walk along the rails. Quickly, on the slope, twisting my ankles, tripping on the sleepers. I run, I run and my feet are coated in screams.

10

Ploughing Through the Night

I say goodbye to my father's twin. Mouths twist into the shapes of dry kisses.

My uncle stands in the middle of the street.

I read backwards.

I have the wide eyes of a person leaving.

Describing the landscape in the narration of my personal drama.

The sensation of being threaded through a needle that embroiders the letters of my name. I take a wide angle shot of the wheat fields.

Fifteen minutes in a straight line, along the ditch, among nettles and stalks swaying in the wind.

A long fall with no landing.

I carry books sentenced to exile.

I plough through the night of this other continent in a fast car, my face as a little girl, as an adult, against the cold back window.

11

Travel Epilogue

Back from my travels, the Atlantic returns everything to its rightful place. I feel as if my life until now has been nothing more than a prologue, that there are many chapters left to write. I take stock of the damage. Some part of me was left floating around those streets, that landscape and those faces that don't belong anywhere. I feel like I didn't fully leave them behind, that I haven't fully returned. I clean out my closet and find one of Dad's old jackets. I rifle through the pockets; I find a piece of stale bread and a picture of myself.

Before my departure, my dad's twin leads me through the city of their childhood, retracing their regular paths, old outings. We spy on the people who now live in what was their first house. I verify the shell encrusted in their second, which Dad and I had seen on TV. I've returned fifty years after he left to take in the same landscape of a city at war.

Dad, I remember you reading the newspaper, lost in the pages, searching between the lines for the story of your childhood. After this trip, I feel like I know and understand you better. But it doesn't matter anymore. I didn't get to say goodbye; you were left with the usual angry silence. My hand still waving an unfin-ished farewell. I cut out images of war, always in black and white, no matter the period. I could talk to you about my personal battles, about the man I loved, the wounds I hold in the centre of my heart. It would help you understand that when I'm distant, absent, staring into space, absorbed in my thoughts, hypnotised by my books, writing feverishly in my journals, it's because I too am fighting my own war.

I look through my photos of the trip. I stop on one of a man I don't know, looking outside the frame. In the city of cathedrals. He's telling me something with his eyes. It's strange, he's in the clearest corner of the photo. The rest of the image is flooded with light. I know that I focused on him unintentionally, but he's there, staring at me with his black eyes. It's like he bewitched my camera as it captured his angular face, shrouding his image in a halo of mystery. He dominates the depth of field; the foreground is blurry.

I remember that day in the darkroom. I place the negative in the tray and carefully submerge it. Forms begin to appear, contrasts. I start to make out a body. The intruder gradually materialises. The fixative brings him to life. I amplify him for a better look. The man stands in the corner of the shot, dropping off the edge of my panoramic view. I'd like to ask him about the judgement I see in his eyes. I carry the photo between the pages of my planner; I haven't showed it to anyone. I look at it every night so that, in the daytime, I can search for him on my way to work, on the subway, at the airport, from my window, in my dreams.

Who are you? With your subversive smile. We're experts in wreckage, surrounded by ruins and shards. You also hate crowds and look in from the outside at gatherings. You stand like me, at the edge of everything, even my photo. You're another shadow in the corner at parties, observing the empty glasses, the furniture pushed against the walls and the rugs rolled up. You're the part of me that was left behind on that other continent. That other half I should go back to find.

12

Occupied Dream

Early in the morning I dial the house on the palm-lined avenue. You never forget your childhood phone number. It's busy. I hang up. I dial again. The voice of a little girl answers and I'm scared it might be me on the other end of the line.

I open my planner. There's the photo of the stranger. I stare at the image as if waiting for it to reveal the man's identity. Because, after all, it's the open letter I'm writing, the excuse I'm inventing to return. A photo I carry as I try to avoid the afternoon sun. I stare at him. A man photographed by chance looks me in the eye. What does he see? I replace Franz's picture on my nightstand. I talk to him before I turn off the light and fall asleep. Are we the memory of someone we've forgotten?

I walk, I remember. I'm Tamara. I made a small change in my bedroom. I'm Tamara. I'm walking to work. I walk against the current. I have to break the silence.

13

Delayed Response

My uncle writes to say he's dying.

That a plum has ripened bluish in his armpit.

That he's leaving me his only cherished possessions: his pocket watch and his collection of porcelain dogs.

The precariousness of the hustle and bustle of everyday urgency.

Living among bombs, men divided between front lines and hiding places.

The new post-war poverty, homes and belongings lost, out on the streets. His furniture is moved out on a muggy afternoon, the slanting sun filling the narrow room, where nothing will ever be the same.

I'm afraid that every question might contain an answer I won't recognise.

I set a glass of water on my folded response. The words are spaced out, the letters smear, an ink stain seeps across a page splattered with signs, plans shattered against a wall. The last letter arrives after his death.

14

Backstage

I'm in the dressing room, overcome with fear. I don't want to look out at the audience, to see the faces of the spectators. Backstage, I pull the strings of the puppets who tell the story that floods my mind in the shower, on my way to and from work, whenever my mind wanders or as I turn the pages of the newspaper.

I've already peeked through the curtains. It's nothing like the days offstage: it's an improvisation of the moments as they come, filtered through the diaphragm, a photograph, wrought-iron bars, or a window or a door. Choosing an image as a guide and drawing a path that will lead to it. Cherishing an object created for a still life. Looking sidelong at the familiar. We explore the topography of the land. Through memory, events may occur a second time, a third. The pages rewrite themselves again and again. Centripetal movements dissolve past forms as soon as they're revealed. Personal maps are carefully drawn and coloured in. Landscapes provide scale, distance, colours, and light.

Who will I be after the curtain falls and the words THE END are written? What will become of us? We're not even alive yet. After this, what's left? Someone moves around making final plans. A text drafted in many languages. The corner where I'm supposed to stand is too narrow. I take my place among the other members of the cast. We must all unfurl our narratives, our personal cartographies. I repeat my character's description, each of her traits, her motto. One, two, three. I take a deep breath and leave the stage. Someone declares that something has ended, that something has begun. The story not only restores time, but space as well.

15

Staging

The heavy curtains part. It's opening night. The vast stage is illuminated. The cast delivers surprises. We perform for the first time in the presence of others. We've memorised our lines and the expressions that distinguish us. Our labyrinths have led us out.

The characters stand in the wings, walk to the edge of the stage. My mother appears from between the heavy velvet veils. She shuffles her feet, her wrists are bandaged and she stops at centre stage. She wears heavy makeup. Her eyes are lined. Her face looks terse, her features well-defined. Mum has recovered her beauty. She bats her long curly lashes, but her cheekbones have fallen slightly. She retouches her lipstick. Mum has dyed her hair blonde; it suits her. She wears the shirt I gave her. She doesn't scream, she doesn't scream, she doesn't scream. She tells me she hasn't been sick in a long time. She looks at me differently, she looks at me. She takes a comb from her purse. She begins to brush my hair, earning my forgiveness as she combs from root to tip. She hums a melody in her throat. Her expression changes. She looks tired.

My brother and sister enter hand in hand, thin, lovely, bright-eyed. They move to opposite ends of the stage and a blue light bathes their faces. Dad enters from the other side. He limps, walking with difficulty; he smiles slightly, showing his missing teeth. The hem of his trousers is undone and he wears a hat tilted on his bald head. He carries a thick newspaper wedged under his arm. Behind him his twin appears, Dad times two. He holds an open map. In his pocket he carries a porcelain dog.

Dad climbs onto my shoulders. I carry him. He's heavy. My collarbone compresses under his weight. My back and neck tense. I turn and Dad turns with me. I walk across the stage. I move from one side to the other. I turn in slow motion. Riding atop me, Dad doesn't want to get down. I walk to the centre of the stage with him still on my shoulders.

Waiting in the wings are the two important men in my life. They stand side by side, in chronological order. It's Franz's turn. He enters dressed as a groom, but barefoot. His bony feet shuffle over the boards with long creaking sounds. His face is a clean surface where another story could be written. He carries an empty suitcase in one hand; in the other, a page with incomprehensible scrawls. I don't know the second man yet. He's the guy from the photo, with blurred features, a piercing gaze. He remains at the edge of the stage.

I hug the stranger from the photo. He's left the corner of the picture. He moves to the centre and offers me a crooked smile. I stand beside him. He studies my soft roundness, a section of my dress, a shoe, the corner of my suitcase. I write about a train that leaves and returns to the same place. One day, I think, I'll go back to that country, that other continent. The man's mysterious image is the open link that forces me back to close the chain. I have to wrap up my story. And you'll be waiting for me there.

I'm Davor. I demand a different part. My character is too far in the background. Please. I'm too nervous to say my lines. To finish this sentence. I speak quickly and don't know what to say. I designed this theatre. No one listens to me; I speak too quietly. I don't know why I move my hands. I think I'm going to be famous. I am.

I'm Tamara. I'm me. I want to be invisible. I want to live under a table. I want to clean out my closet. Time is vertical for me. In my memory, events occur a second time, a third. I'm afraid of melting into a stain as I sleep. My loneliness moves aside when I lie down in bed. Who wants to brush my hair? Who wants to look after my watch and my porcelain dogs? I am.

I'm Dad. I read in a foreign language. I take shelter in an alphabet without history. I'm always thirsty. A tram rumbles through my head. I'm stuck facing the wrong direction. I step in my father's blood and stand up. I'm gone.

I'm Franz. I'm not to be trusted; I look through your things when you're not there. I have a hole in my heart. I search the back corners of the city. Test the mechanical limits of death. My desire has a rough edge. Where did I leave my shoes? I'm barefoot. I'm gone.

I'm the uncle. I hear the kitchen door. I hear the whisper of the tap. I hear the buzz of the refrigerator. I hear the clinking of the silverware. You guys are eating. You haven't called me to the table. I've stolen from the dead. Do dogs bark in photographs? I'm gone.

I'm Adela. I'm the daughter of another man, a man who doesn't have a part in this play. I've spent too much time looking at his photos. My legs are falling asleep. It's strange to stand here alongside you all. But I am.

I'm Mum. Despite the screaming. Despite my forgetting. Despite the illnesses. I love my trio of sad shadows. I lie on the railway sleepers. Despite that, I'm pretty. And I am.

I don't know why I talk with my hands. I heard the buzz of the refrigerator. I'm too nervous to remember my lines. I think I'm going to be famous. Despite everything.

I want to organise my closet. Time is vertical for me. My loneliness moves aside when I lie down in bed. I hear the kitchen door. Despite my forgetting. Do dogs bark in photos. I am. A tram rumbles through my head. I'm stuck facing the wrong direction. I hear the clinking of the silverware. In my memory, events occur a second time, a third. I step in my father's blood and stand up. I hear the buzz of the refrigerator. Despite the screaming. I'm stuck facing the wrong direction.

Our overlapping monologues float up to the dome of the theatre. We rewrite each other's parts. We bring our characters to life. The director stops the scene. Our characters pause. He examines us and corrects our postures. The performance loses momentum as we try out new poses and expressions. The scene deteriorates. We know the show is no longer the same.

The curtain falls. The audience applauds and cheers. Those of us on stage don't know what to do. We fidget awkwardly. From up here we see only anonymous heads, black dots. Then we look at each other. We bow and take each other's hands, all of us gripping, for an instant, the same lifeline.

CHARCO PRESS

Director & Editor: Carolina Orloff
Director: Samuel McDowell

www.charcopress.com

Theatre of War was published on
80gsm Munken Premium Cream paper.

The text was designed using Bembo 11.5 and ITC Galliard.

Printed in July 2020 by TJ International
Padstow, Cornwall, PL28 8RW using responsibly sourced paper
and environmentally-friendly adhesive.

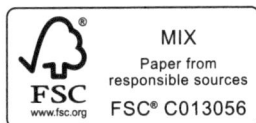